The ADVENTURE IS NOW

The ADVENTURE IS NOW

Jess Redman

FARRAR STRAUS GIROUX · NEW YORK

Farrar Straus Giroux Books for Young Readers
An imprint of Macmillan Children's Publishing Group, LLC
120 Broadway, New York, NY 10271

Text copyright © 2021 by Jessica Redman
All rights reserved
Printed in the United States of America
Designed by Cassie Gonzales
Interior illustrations © 2021 by Cassie Gonzales

First edition, 2021

ISBN 978-0-374-31471-2

10 9 8 7 6 5 4 3 2 1

mackids.com

Library of Congress Cataloging-in-Publication Data is available.

Our books may be purchased in bulk for promotional, educational, or business use. Please
contact your local bookseller or the Macmillan Corporate and Premium Sales Department at
(800) 221-7945 ext. 5442 or by email at MacmillanSpecialMarkets@macmillan.com.

For Russ

You are seriously, supremely, completely,

wonderfully spectaculous, and

my favorite adventure story is ours.

The ADVENTURE IS NOW

Now or never! You must live in the present,
launch yourself on every wave,
find your eternity in each moment.
Fools stand on their island opportunities
and look toward another land.
There is no other land; there is no
other life but this . . .

—Henry David Thoreau

CHAPTER 1

A Letter for Milton P. Greene

On June 3 of the Most Totally, Terribly, Horribly, Heinously Rotten Year of All Time, a letter was delivered to Milton P. Greene's house. The envelope had probably been white once, but now it was a sort of phlegmy green, and it was covered in about a hundred stamps. That letter had traveled a long, long way.

Only moments after the letter's arrival, a bus pulled up at the corner.

And even before the doors could fully open, Milton P. Greene squeezed himself out onto the sidewalk and took off running.

From behind him, he could hear someone calling, "See you tomorrow, Elaina!"

"Bye, Nico!" someone else shouted.

"So long!" Milton hollered over his shoulder. "Until we meet again!"

No one yelled *So long, Milton!* back, but he hadn't really expected anyone to. Milton had been practically so-longless for the entire Most Totally, Terribly, Horribly, Heinously Rotten Year of All Time and completely so-longless since the Bird Brain Incident.

As expected as it was, the silence still felt like some great, invisible hand reaching out from the bus and shoving him forward, shoving him away. Milton stumbled, then raced on, a small, pale bespectacled blur with an oversize backpack beelining toward home.

Where the letter was waiting.

But when Milton reached his house, he didn't take so much as a peek inside the mailbox that hung beneath the doorbell. He didn't see the bills or the credit card offers or the dental-cleaning reminder (*We miss seeing your smile!*)—or the phlegmy-green envelope.

He flung open his front door and threw himself inside.

The house that Milton ran through was empty. His mother had been working more and more lately, but she'd told him she would be home at 5:50, and she was a very punctual lady.

His father, however, would not be coming home at 5:50 or 6:15 or midnight or ever. He had moved out three months ago, and now Milton only saw him on Tuesday afternoons and every other weekend.

Milton's former best friend, Dev, who used to go on backyard expeditions and play video games with him after school, wouldn't be coming over either. Dev had hardly spoken to Milton since November.

Yes, it had been a rough year. It had been the Most Totally, Terribly, Horribly, Heinously Rotten Year of All Time.

Except for one thing.

The thing that Milton was running to.

Isle of Wild.

In his room, Milton collapsed onto his bed and pulled his HandHeld out from under his pillow. He had finally convinced his parents to buy him the HandHeld last summer, when things had already begun to get a little rotten around the edges. He used to sneak it to school every day, but after the Bird Brain Incident, his mother started checking his backpack before he left to catch the bus. She didn't always remember, but she had remembered this morning, much to his dismay.

Breathless, Milton jabbed at the *Power* button. Then he pressed the green-eyed-bobcat icon.

It seemed to take too long, it seemed to take forever, but then—

Isle of Wild's opening story began.

Sea Hawk Ferox, Naturalist and Explorer Extraordinaire, came bursting onto the screen. Dashing, brawny, and brilliant, Sea Hawk had been en route to the Flora & Fauna Federation headquarters when his ship had capsized in a raging tempest. He had washed ashore on an uninhabited island where he found a most unusual mixture of flora and fauna, including umbrellabirds, corpse flowers, aardvarks, and a miniature green-eyed bobcat that he named Dear Lady DeeDee.

Instead of trying to escape from the island, Sea Hawk (somehow still sporting his signature straw hat with a peacock feather tucked in the band) had opened his (somehow not waterlogged) field journal and set off into the underbrush with his new feline friend.

On the HandHeld's screen now, Sea Hawk was leaping out of a towering redwood, DeeDee perched on his shoulder, binoculars around his neck.

"The adventure is now!" he cried, his voice deep and booming and chock-full of awesomeness.

"The adventure is now," Milton agreed. "And boy, am I ready."

With a lung-emptying sigh of relief, Milton shed his skinny, bespectacled, Bird-Brained, un-so-longed, soon-to-be-divorce-parented skin and became Sea Hawk—dashing, brawny, and brilliant.

It was the best feeling he'd had all day.

He didn't know that twenty feet away, a message from another island was waiting.

The Lone Island.

He didn't know that an adventure was just around the corner.

Not an adventure for Sea Hawk.

An adventure for Milton P. Greene.

CHAPTER 2

Mortal Peril

On June 4 of the Most Totally, Terribly, Horribly, Heinously Rotten Year of All Time, at exactly 5:52, Milton P. Greene's mother handed him the letter from the Lone Island.

Well, she tried to, anyway. Milton was in his room again, lying on his bed playing *Isle of Wild*. And *Isle of Wild* required two hands.

"Milton, turn that off for a minute," said Milton's father.

Since Milton's father had not set foot inside the house in three months, his inexplicable presence was enough to make Milton jerk his head up in surprise. As soon as he did, however, there was a howl of pain from the HandHeld.

"I definitely will," Milton said, returning his gaze to the screen, "as soon as Sea Hawk is out of mortal peril."

Sea Hawk was currently being pursued by the huge-eyed, many-appendaged cephalopod he had been observing. While Sea Hawk carried a machete in his utility belt, he didn't use it on the island's fauna. He was a naturalist, after all. He explored and studied and researched. He did not de-appendage.

So instead, Milton was frantically button-pressing and joystick-jiggling to make Sea Hawk duck, twist, and emit his signature bird-of-prey call in an attempt to intimidate the creature. Milton knew from a vast wealth of *Isle of Wild* experience that if he so much as blinked, Sea Hawk would be a goner for sure.

"Mighty moles and voles!" yelled the feather-hatted naturalist as a bright red tentacle snaked around his throat. Milton increased his rate of button-pressing and joystick-jiggling.

Milton's mother, seemingly oblivious to Sea Hawk's plight, reached over and plucked the HandHeld from Milton's grasp.

"Mighty moles and voles!" Milton cried, making a desperate grab for the device. "At least pause it. You've almost certainly killed me!"

"We have some wonderful news," Milton's mother replied firmly. She held out the letter again. "You'll want to read this."

There had been zero wonderful news this year, and Milton was 99.99 percent sure that whatever was inside the envelope was not going to change that.

But even though he was leaning as far from the letter as he could and even though he was staring unblinkingly at the little screen in his mother's hand and *only* at that screen, his parents were not getting the hint.

"Take the letter," his father urged. "It's for you. Uncle Evan sent it all the way from the Lone Island."

Milton gasped and pressed his hands to his heart. The Lone Island, he knew, was an itty-bitty, teeny-tiny, super-duper-remote island in the middle of the Atlantic, much like the Isle of Wild. Milton's uncle was a naturalist who ran research studies there, much like Sea Hawk (except not nearly as brawny or dashing . . . also, not shipwrecked). Milton had only met Uncle Evan one time, back when he was five years old, and he had *never* been to the Lone Island, but once upon a time, it had been his favorite place in the whole entire world.

"In that case," he said, "perhaps I'll have a look."

CHAPTER 3

The Lone Island Letter

Inside that phlegmy-green, stamp-covered envelope, there was a slightly cleaner piece of notebook paper with a few pen-scrawled lines. Milton adjusted his glasses and read:

Dear Milton,

I'm looking forward to your visit. It's pretty tricky to get here, so I arranged your flights. I'm enclosing the itinerary.

I'll be waiting for you at the airstrip. See you on June 8.

Uncle Evan

P.S. Tell your dad the Incredible Symphonic Cicadas should be emerging soon, and this might be his last chance to hear them.

Behind the letter was a paper filled with flight numbers and times and finally, at the very bottom, these words: *ARRIVAL: The Lone Island.*

"Can this possibly mean what I think it means?" Milton asked. His parents both wore huge, frozen smiles—the kind of smile you smile when you're trying to convince someone that a letter contains wonderful news.

"It means you're going to the Lone Island for the summer!" Milton's father cried, sounding peppier than he had all year. "You get to stay with Uncle Evan."

"It'll be like visiting a real *Isle of Wild*," Milton's mother added.

Milton glanced back and forth between them, openmouthed and bug-eyed. "Well, that's—that's very—egad. Really?"

"You've been wanting to go there ever since Uncle Evan's visit," his father replied. "Remember?"

Of course Milton remembered. During that visit seven years ago, Uncle Evan had taken Milton and his parents birdwatching and hiking and even camping. Over roasted marshmallows, he had told them about his life on the nearly deserted Lone Island and about the island's famous explorer, Dr. Ada Paradis. Dr. Paradis claimed the island's jungle was filled with never-before-seen creatures like a pachyderm that burrowed underground, a tree that shot poison arrows, a bird with stars in its tail feathers, and thousands more just waiting to be found. And Uncle Evan had been sure, absolutely sure, that he would find them all.

That visit had been the start of Milton's Nature Phase. His parents had gotten him a pair of neon-green binoculars with seagull decals on the sides, and he had spent many an after-school hour in their row house's minuscule backyard cataloging types of grass and peering up at pigeons and crows. On Sundays, Milton and his parents (and sometimes Dev) would head to a local park. These expeditions had been the highlight of Milton's week, and he had been pretty sure they were the highlight of his parents' week too.

Yes, if he'd gotten this letter a year ago, back in fifth grade, Milton would have wept tears of joy. But things had changed. His parents hadn't offered to take him on an expedition in months, and he hadn't asked. His Nature Phase was over.

"I *used* to want to go there," Milton said. "I'm not entirely certain that I still do."

"This is a once-in-a-lifetime opportunity." His mother hadn't stopped smiling, but Milton could hear the impatience that had become nearly constant this year creeping into her voice. "And your father and I, we need—we need some time to sort things out."

"You mean . . . getting-back-together things?" Milton asked, even though he knew the answer.

Milton's father shook his head. Milton's mother stopped smiling.

"No, Milton," she said softly. "The opposite is what I mean."

Now Milton understood.

The opposite. Like his father cleaning out the last of his stuff.

Like finalizing the custody plan. Like divorcing, completely, at last, for good. The End.

And they didn't want him here while that happened.

The kids at school, they didn't want him here. Not even Dev, who mostly pretended he didn't exist.

No one wanted him here.

So long, Milton.

"Well, that is a very tempting offer," he said. He folded up the itinerary and the letter and replaced them in the envelope. "And I truly do hate to disappoint Uncle Evan, but unfortunately, I must decline."

From the corner of his eye, Milton could see his parents exchanging glances—say-something, no-you-say-something glances—but neither of them spoke, and when Milton reached for his HandHeld, his mother gave it to him.

He had been right though. When the screen lit back up, Sea Hawk was dead. Milton would have to start over.

"I have plans with Sea Hawk this summer," he said. He pressed *Restart*, and the shipwrecked naturalist sprung back to life. "I'm not going anywhere."

"Onward! Ever onward!" Sea Hawk bellowed.

"Indeed," Milton agreed.

But as he maneuvered Sea Hawk toward the bay where the territorial cephalopod was once again hiding in the shallows, Milton had this (very disturbing) thought: This was the first time in months that his parents had been together in the same room without biting each other's heads off.

If they'd been willing to do this, if they'd been willing to work together and smile and be as patient and peppy as possible—well, then they really might mean business.

Milton might be going to the Lone Island.

CHAPTER 4

Business

As it turned out, they did mean business.

The next day, which was the last day of school, Milton's father was waiting for him at the bus stop. In spite of Milton's very emphatic initial protests, his father drove them to the outdoor store, where they spent the afternoon picking out hiking boots and a utility belt and a brand-new field journal and even a straw hat with a peacock feather tucked in its band. It was, Milton had to admit, a truly magnificent piece of headwear, and he hadn't seen his father smile so much in a long time.

"You're going to have the best trip, Milt," his father said when they pulled up to the house afterward. "I can't wait to hear about it."

The next day, which was the day before he was supposed to fly out, Milton's mother didn't work from her home office or on her phone like she usually did on Saturdays. Instead she helped Milton pack his belongings into a canvas backpack.

Well, actually, mostly *she* packed his belongings, while Milton (wearing his magnificent headwear) tried to talk her out of packing his belongings.

"This summer is going to be just what you need," she said before she left his room for the night. Her voice wasn't one bit impatient, and her hands were on his shoulders, her eyes searching for his under the brim of his lowered hat. "What we all need. I promise."

After she left, Milton couldn't sleep. That wasn't unusual though. At night, in the darkness and silence, with his HandHeld turned off, Milton's thoughts turned on.

Thoughts about how his father was living downtown in an apartment now.

Thoughts about how his parents had snapped and spat out words (and sometimes even yelled them) before his father had moved into that downtown apartment.

Thoughts about the Bird Brain Incident and his former best friend, Dev.

Totally, terribly, horribly, heinously rotten thoughts.

Most nights, Milton tried to distract himself from all that rottenness with *Isle of Wild* scenarios. He would imagine that he was Sea Hawk scaling to the spidery-frond tops of palm trees to pluck coconuts or being brought offerings of decapitated lizards by Dear

14

Lady DeeDee, who would then meow-snarl words in a language only he could understand. Pretending to be Sea Hawk didn't always help him fall asleep, but it was better than being Milton P. Greene.

But tonight, try as he might, he could not distract himself. Tonight, he couldn't stop thinking about how he did not want to be sent halfway around the world.

And he couldn't stop thinking about how he sort of *did* want to be sent halfway around the world.

His thoughts were loud and jumbly and terrified and eager and achy, and when he finally fell asleep, he still had not come anywhere close to sorting them out.

CHAPTER 5

Milton En Route

Milton's thoughts remained a smooshey mishmash of a mess the next morning as his mother drove him to the airport, where his father met them. They went through security together and then to the terminal, and before Milton knew it, his parents were hugging him goodbye and a flight attendant was guiding him down the gangway.

He was on his way to the Lone Island, whether he wanted to be or not.

That first flight took Milton across the country on a medium-size plane. He played *Isle of Wild* and sipped grape soda from a tiny plastic cup. That was all the flight attendants would give him even though he made several (very eloquent, in his opinion) requests for the full can. He had never flown before and, aside from the grape soda–stinginess and his many reservations about the trip itself, he found aviation life to be quite enjoyable.

The next flight was overnight and took Milton out of the country on a huge plane with a tiny TV on the back of each seat and eight blue-water toilets. He tried a new tactic this time: He told the flight attendants that his parents didn't want him anymore and were sending him to live on a deserted island, which was almost-kind-of-sort-of true. He wasn't sure if the flight attendants believed him or not, but they gave him one of those baby-size pillows, a blanket, and as many cans of grape soda as he wanted (he wanted seven). He snuggled into his seat, slurped his drinks, and played *Isle of Wild* some more, pressing *Restart* every time Sea Hawk met yet another untimely end.

The third and final ticket was for a supply-filled biplane that was so rusty and rattly Milton was absolutely positive it was one milli-second away from bursting into a thousand pieces and launching him into the smack-dab center of the Atlantic Ocean.

"Mighty moles and voles! I want to go back to the mainland," he groaned as grape soda tidal-waved in his stomach. There weren't any airsickness bags in the supply plane, so he kept his new explorer hat at the ready, and his HandHeld safely tucked away in his bag.

He wished he had protested more.

17

He wished he had locked the door to his room and refused to come out.

He wished he was still in fifth grade with a best friend and married parents.

He groaned and wished and kept his explorer hat under his chin until—

"Look out your window!" called the pilot, who seemed entirely too calm considering the extreme danger they were in.

Milton looked. And there it was: the Lone Island.

The island rose up out of the sea like a green jewel, bright and lush and—

Moving! For half a second, it looked like the entire island was in motion, shivering and writhing, like something growing, like something alive.

"Great flapping falcons!" Milton cried, nose pressed to the window. "What is the meaning of—AHHH!"

The plane had begun to descend.

Down, down, down the biplane sputtered and jerked, down toward the long strip of concrete on the far side of the Lone Island, where it came to a teeth-shattering landing that flung everything— crates, mailbags, straw-hatted passengers—around the cabin.

"Have we arrived?" gasped Milton P. Greene from the floor of the plane.

CHAPTER 6

Ahoy, Uncle Evan

The pilot hopped right out of the plane, but Milton spent a few moments lying flat on his back, catching his breath. Then he staggered to his feet, gathered his scattered belongings, and disembarked. He was extremely relieved to be back on solid ground. He was also extremely relieved he hadn't puked in his new hat, because the sun was very, very bright, and also because he really liked that hat.

As promised, Uncle Evan was there waiting. Standing under the shade of a coconut-laden palm tree, he wore a once-white T-shirt and a floppy (not nearly as awesome as Milton's or Sea Hawk's) hat. He had sun-weathered skin and streaks of gray in his black beard. He was small and bespectacled and, to be entirely honest, not nearly as impressive as Milton had pictured him for the past seven years.

"Ahoy, Uncle Evan!" Milton called. "Am I ever glad to see you. You're shorter than I remember though."

"You're taller," Uncle Evan said. He spoke quietly, and the corners of his mouth turned up into the smallest of smiles. "How were the flights?"

"Horrendous," Milton replied. "Horrific. Really, really awful."

"That bad, huh?"

"I have a very sensitive stomach," Milton said. "Also, I wasn't exactly on board with this summer-on-the-Lone-Island plan."

"Is that right? Well, you look like you're *dressed* for summer on the Lone Island," Uncle Evan said, taking in Milton's ensemble: many-pocketed pants that unzipped into shorts, a patch-covered vest (including a patch for the Flora & Fauna Federation), hiking boots, and a utility belt—complete with water bottle, flashlight, air horn, penknife, waterproof watch, matches, and various and sundry other wilderness-trekking necessities. Milton hadn't been able to persuade his father to buy him the very expensive Magnifycent2000s at the outdoor store, so his old, neon-green plastic binoculars hung around his neck.

"Purchasing this gear was part of my parents' cunning ploy to convince me to come here willingly," Milton told him. "In spite of that, I'm very fond of it. And look—they even got me this extremely authentic field journal." He yanked a notebook from one of his pants pockets and held it up for his uncle to admire.

"That's a real naturalist's journal," Uncle Evan said with an approving nod. "I bet you'll need it this summer too. There's a lot to explore here." He paused to squint up at the sky. "We better get going. You're a little late, and the sun sets fast this close to the equator."

Milton followed Uncle Evan down a steep and, frankly, quite treacherous palm tree–lined path. In no time, he was sweating, and there were a million bugs buzzing around his head (three of which actually flew *into his mouth!*). Since his sun exposure had been nearly zilch this year, he was sure that his decidedly pasty skin was turning lobster-red. It was a relief when he spotted a concrete-block building tucked into the foliage.

"Is that your house?" he asked. "Can we go inside and sit down for about twenty hours?"

"That's the research station," Uncle Evan said over his shoulder. "I do most of my work there, along with a small team of scientists. Everyone's already gone for the day, but you'll meet them around the island tomorrow."

Milton tried to say *I'm sure that will be delightful*, but it came out as a gaspy groan.

"We're almost there," Uncle Evan assured him. "See? The docks are right up ahead."

With the research station behind them, Milton could now make

21

out a glimmer of deep aquamarine, a flash of frothy white, and then, a few steps later, a weather-beaten dock came into view.

"Why do we need docks?" Milton asked. "Aren't we here?"

"The cottages are on the other side of the island," Uncle Evan explained. "We have to take my boat."

It seemed that Milton's time on solid ground was already over.

CHAPTER 7

Blergh!

After five minutes at sea, Milton was clutching his stomach and groaning again. His only consolation was that at least his beautiful new hat would be spared; he had the whole ocean to puke in.

Uncle Evan tried his best to distract him. "I know you were probably a bit nervous about coming here," he said as he navigated the motorboat toward open water. "It does take some getting used to—being so remote. That's one of the reasons the Lone Island was uninhabited and unexplored until Dr. Paradis arrived fifty years ago. Do you remember me telling you about Dr. Paradis?"

"Urgh!" Milton groaned.

Uncle Evan seemed to take that as a no. "She passed away not too long after I came to visit you," he said, raising his voice to be heard over the rush of wind and waves. "Before she came here, she'd discovered thousands of new species, explored some of the most inaccessible corners of the world, and published dozens of books and papers."

"Argh!" Milton moaned.

"She was fascinated by this island though," Uncle Evan continued. "For centuries, travelers and explorers and pirates and developers had tried to turn it into all sorts of things—a new country, a resort, a military station. But something about the wildlife on this island made it impossible to live here, and eventually, every one of them gave up and left. Except Dr. Paradis."

"Blergh!" Milton cried.

Uncle Evan nodded in agreement. "Yes, she was brilliant," he said. "Way more brilliant than me. I've been here nine years, and I still haven't figured this island out. Maybe you can help me though, Milt. What do you think?"

What Milton would have said (had the contents of his churning stomach not been creeping up his esophagus) was that he wasn't entirely sure how much help he was going to be and were they almost there because his gut situation was getting dire, but all he could manage was, "Glergh!"

Then Uncle Evan swung the little motorboat around, and the east side of the island came into view.

"Would you look at that!" Milton leaped to his feet and pressed his neon-green binoculars to his eyes, stomach woes forgotten.

"Hey—Milton—sit down!" cried Uncle Evan as the boat lurched from side to side.

Milton did not sit down. He stood, balancing with one arm outstretched in the salt-brimmed and sun-warmed southern Atlantic wind.

Ahead of them was a half-moon bay with jagged rock formations jutting out of sparkling turquoise water. A crescent of sandy beach gave way to seagrass-covered dunes with three thatch-roofed cottages spread out along them. Then, beyond the cottages, a palm tree–filled jungle rose up, dense and green and fit for any explorer. Surrounding it all was a sky ablaze with sunset light.

It was like a scene out of *Isle of Wild* rendered in perfect, unpixelated color.

Or like something Milton had dreamed about during the Nature Phase, before the Most Totally, Terribly, Horribly, Heinously Rotten Year of All Time, back when he had wanted nothing more than to travel to this barely charted, hardly explored island in the middle of the ocean.

And now here he was.

"Ahoy, Lone Island!" Milton cried. "Ahoy!"

CHAPTER 8

Spaghetti and Meatballs

The sunset was as rapid as Uncle Evan had predicted, and it was totally dark by the time they motored up to the island's dock. As Milton clambered out of the boat, the only sounds were the chirping of bugs and the hushing of waves and the whoosh of the wind.

Inside Uncle Evan's cottage, there were two rooms separated by a curtain of wooden beads. In the dim glow of the oil lamp (the only source of light), Milton saw that the main room had a couch, lots of mostly empty, homemade-looking shelves, and a splintery driftwood table. There was a door leading to the bathroom, which Uncle Evan explained had a composting toilet and a rain-barrel shower.

"Are you hungry?" he asked after the tour, which had taken approximately thirty seconds.

Milton plopped down on one of the stools by the driftwood

table. "Famished," he said. "And I've never been so tired, not ever in my entire life."

"I bet," Uncle Evan said. He opened a window, then popped the top on a family-size can of spaghetti and meatballs and dumped it into a dented-up pot on a camp stove. "I wish I could spend the day with you tomorrow, but I actually have to take the boat back to the research station. I'm in the middle of a project that . . . well, it can't be put on hold. You could come with me—"

"No, thank you," Milton replied. "Solid ground for me."

Uncle Evan laughed a very out-of-practice laugh. It sounded more like choking and ended in him clearing his throat.

"I'm sure you'll find plenty to do." He took two bowls down from the shelf above the hot plate. "You can swim in the bay, hike into the jungle—well, at least until the Truth-Will-Out Vine gets too thick."

"What's Truth-Will-Out Vine?" Milton asked.

"Probably the main reason so many travelers and explorers and pirates and investors didn't stick around here," Uncle Evan replied. "You'll see it tomorrow—you can't miss it. The vine covers the entire interior of the island, and we think it's probably destroyed the plant and animal life beneath it. It's incredibly fast-growing and stronger than any plant I've ever encountered." He paused for a moment, his wooden spoon scraping against the bottom of the battered pot as he stirred his culinary masterpiece. "Listen, I don't know if you even

27

remember me saying this, but I guess I should tell you that I haven't discovered any never-before-seen species like I thought I would."

Milton had been slumped with exhaustion, but now he straightened up. "What about the ones Dr. Paradis told you about? The underground pachyderm and the star-feathered bird and the tree with the poison arrows—have you found them?"

"No," Uncle Evan replied, head hung low. "I haven't. I don't—I haven't really found much of anything except the Truth-Will-Out Vine."

"Oh. I see," Milton said. He picked at the wood slivers in the table, exhaustion and now disappointment weighing him down again. "I guess it doesn't matter. I'm not in my Nature Phase anymore. I don't know if I'll even do much nature expeditioning while I'm here—other than the virtual kind, that is."

"You say that," Uncle Evan said, "but I saw how excited you were when we came up to the island. And you've got your explorer gear." He plopped a scoop of spaghetti into each bowl. "You remind me of myself when I showed up here nine years ago actually. Who knows, maybe you'll be the one who finds those creatures."

"Perhaps you speak the truth," Milton replied, head now on the table, "but I highly doubt it."

After dinner, Milton used the kind-of-weird bathroom, then watched as Uncle Evan set up the pull-out couch.

"You know, Milt," his uncle said, tucking the sheet into place, "your dad told me you've been having a rough year. I'm actually— well, I'm having a rough year myself. A rough few years, to be honest." He smoothed the sheet and gave Milton the smallest of smiles. "But I'm glad you're here."

The words seemed to come through a fog that Milton could no longer shake. When Uncle Evan tossed him a pillow, Milton's arms didn't even leave his sides. The pillow smacked him in the face and landed on the mattress, and Milton followed it.

"Thank you, my good man," he murmured, curling up on the couch-bed.

His eyes were closed, but he heard his uncle turning down the wick of the oil lamp near the couch and tiptoeing from the room. The beaded curtain clink-clinked as Uncle Evan passed through, and soon there was the sound of breathing getting slower and deeper, slower and deeper until—snores such as Milton had never heard before! Like a hyena laugh mixed with a walrus grunt mixed with a kangaroo cough.

Milton was suddenly wide awake. And as he lay in this strange room listening to his uncle's earsplitting inhalations, he discovered, much to his dismay, that his rotten thoughts had followed him across the ocean.

So he took out his HandHeld, and he turned on *Isle of Wild*.

"The adventure is now!" Sea Hawk roared, crashing through the underbrush.

Milton was too wiped out to agree out loud, but he button-pressed and joystick-jiggled until his exhaustion overwhelmed him and forced his bleary eyes closed.

CHAPTER 9

Ever Onward

Milton was usually an early riser, but he slept late the next morning because it turned out traveling for twenty-six hours straight on three airplanes (one of which had almost certainly nearly plummeted into the ocean on numerous occasions) was extremely exhausting. He slept and slept and slept so hard that when he woke up his face was covered in sleep lines and there was a puddle of drool on his pillow.

Uncle Evan was gone, but there was a note on the silver icebox that read:

Milton,

I didn't want to wake you. I'm heading to the research station, but I'll be back for dinner. Help yourself to anything on the shelves.

Uncle Evan

While he ate a breakfast of canned spaghetti and meatballs (which appeared to be Uncle Evan's sole source of sustenance), Milton considered his plans for the day. Uncle Evan seemed to think he'd be gallivanting about outdoors from dawn till dusk. While Milton *did* plan to go on a brief expedition or two this summer, the only thing he wanted to do right now was get back to *Isle of Wild*.

He retrieved his HandHeld from the couch-bed, but when he pressed the *Power* button, the screen remained blank.

The battery was dead.

Milton glanced around the cottage, searching for an outlet, but he didn't see one right away.

He scanned the walls, every square inch of them.

No luck.

Then he checked the floor and the ceiling and under the couch-bed and even behind the composting toilet.

Still no luck.

The truth came to Milton like a lurch of seasickness. Uncle Evan had done his cooking on a camp stove. The only light was an oil lamp.

This cottage was powerless.

Milton grabbed his HandHeld again, but no matter how many times he pressed (and then jabbed and then mashed) the *Power* button, it didn't turn on.

Milton's thoughts, however, did.

Now that he was no longer traveling, now that he'd had a full night's sleep, the seriousness of his situation was making itself known.

Milton was five thousand miles away from home on a mostly deserted island.

His parents (very nearly Officially Divorced) were halfway across the world.

His former best friend didn't even know where he was (not that he would care).

And if all that wasn't horrendous enough, now he couldn't even play *Isle of Wild.*

It was just him. Alone.

Milton P. Greene.

What was he going to do?

He plunked down onto a stool at the driftwood table. The sun started shining directly into the windows and the air grew stiflingly heavy, but still Milton sat. He sat and stared at his blank HandHeld, wishing as hard as he could that it would turn on because the last thing he wanted to do was spend an entire summer thinking and thinking and thinking about the Most Totally, Terribly, Horribly, Heinously Rotten Year of All Time.

And then his HandHeld *did* turn back on.

There was some kind of blip, a momentary battery surge, and Sea Hawk's voice (distorted but still supremely awesome) belted out, "Onward! Ever onward!"

Milton shoved the screen up to his face. He pressed the *Power* button again and again. Nothing else happened.

But it was enough.

Milton got to his feet. He put on his vest, hiking boots, and utility belt. He hung his neon-green binoculars around his neck, unzipped his pocket-covered pants into shorts, and donned his explorer hat.

There were no mirrors in the cottage, but he took a peek at the top of Uncle Evan's icebox and saw himself peering back. In that blurry surface, he looked like an explorer. He looked like a naturalist.

He looked like Sea Hawk.

He wasn't going to sit in this cottage thinking rotten thoughts for another second.

Sea Hawk had urged him *Onward*, and *Onward* he was going to go.

He was going to find an outlet.

And maybe some of those never-before-seen creatures too.

CHAPTER 10

Check!

The sun was high in the sky and blindingly bright as Milton stepped outside. Tipping his hat low over his eyes, he took in the semicircle of shining water, the rocky beach, the wavy seagrass-covered dunes, and the other two cottages.

Even from Uncle Evan's porch, he could already see plants he recognized—some from his Nature Phase and some from playing *Isle of Wild*. There were palms of every kind, with their feathery fronds fluttering in the gusty sea breeze. There were bumpy ferns, brightly hued blossoms, and winding lianas.

After a few hundred yards, however, everything seemed to become one kind of plant. This, Milton thought, had to be the Truth-Will-Out Vine his uncle had mentioned. The vine, hanging from trees that were completely invisible beneath its strands, formed a bright green wall that extended around the inside of the island as far as Milton could see.

"What a totally terrible vine," he said to himself as he started up the pebbly beach road. "Smothering the island's flora and fauna. Sea Hawk would probably machete it to pieces!" He chopped the air with gusto.

Uncle Evan's cottage had zero decoration. The next cottage had a cheerful yellow door, but the third one was the real eye-catcher. It was covered in a chaotically colorful jungle mural featuring dancing trees, heart-shaped butterflies, and some sort of firefly-fairy creatures. If there was an outlet anywhere, it would be in one of these cottages, but the thought of knocking on a strange door (even one with a laughing rainbow on it) was slightly terrifying, so Milton pressed onward. He would come back later, he reassured himself, after he did a little expeditioning.

During his Nature Phase, Milton used to go on expeditions every chance he got. They were usually in his backyard and they were, in retrospect, incredibly boring (a squirrel sighting was considered a great success). He had done a lot of watching and waiting during his Nature Phase.

In an *Isle of Wild* expedition, on the other hand, it usually took about three and a half seconds before something super amazing appeared (scorpions, jaguars, famished Venus flytraps, a herd of wildebeests, that sort of thing).

Here on the Lone Island, Milton had been expeditioning for at least five minutes and . . . nothing.

Not even a squirrel.

Milton was bored. Milton was hot. He was sure he was getting a sunburn.

Then something brilliant red and dark violet caught his eye, something skittering across the beach—a crab! Pressing his binoculars to his eyes (even though the crab was only four feet away), Milton watched as the many-legged creature darted into a hole between some rocks.

"Egad! What a discovery," Milton said (in his best Sea Hawkian voice). He pulled out his brand-new field journal and turned to the Nature Sightings Checklist in the back. There were a lot of crab species in the Crustacean section—Portunidae, fiddler, ghost, spider. Milton selected *red land crab* after careful consideration and hoped that was the correct choice. He took great satisfaction in making a big red check mark in the box.

Now he was paying attention. Now he noticed the seabirds, some sleek and arrow-like, some improbably awkward and heavy-looking, soaring above. He noticed splashes out in the bay that might have been fish or dolphins or probably even great white sharks. He made a lot of checks on the Marine Life Checklist, some of which were bound to be correct. He even saw a really (kind of) big lizard that could have been (but almost certainly wasn't) a Komodo dragon. He checked the *Komodo dragon* box, just in case.

Forget squirrels! He had never, ever, ever seen so many species in one place. This must be what Sea Hawk felt like constantly, and Milton was getting more sure by the minute that he could, in fact, find a never-before-seen creature. Probably this afternoon.

"Sea Hawk's the name," he said, tipping his hat to a pale yellow spider that he had checked off as a *black widow*. "Wildlife's my ga—AHHH!" The little spider skittered toward Milton. Milton ran.

Other than the harrowing arachnid encounter, it was a surprisingly enjoyable morning. Milton was even a bit disappointed when he found that he had somehow hiked in a great big circle, and was back by Uncle Evan's cottage again.

He was about to head inside when he noticed a trail off the pebbly road that he hadn't seen before. It wasn't a well-worn path like the one he was on, just a place where the dune grass and ferns and trailing vines had been compressed by feet. Human feet probably, but maybe, just maybe (be still, Milton's vest-covered heart!) large animal feet.

If this were *Isle of Wild*, the trail would be a clue. *Go this way* was what the trail would be telling him. And if this were *Isle of Wild*, at the end of that trail there would be wildcats or wild boars or wild some-other-kind-of-crazy-awesome creature.

So, feeling more Sea Hawkian than ever, Milton decided to see where it led.

He trekked through the high grass and into a field of stubby palm trees and sunset-colored wildflowers. He went through a twisty-turny cluster of sea grape trees. Then he came to a sudden stop.

In front of him was the biggest tree he had ever seen.

From playing *Isle of Wild*, Milton knew it was a banyan. The tree had dozens of interconnected trunks and spread out as wide as Milton's house. There were limbs and roots sprawling every which way, and the leafy canopy was dotted with deep red fruits. Built into it, spanning across branch after branch after branch, was a tree house.

Or rather, since it was shaped like an enormous boat, a tree ship.

Behind the tree ship was the thick, bright green Truth-Will-Out Vine.

And coming from the ship were voices.

Boys' voices.

CHAPTER 11

From Bird Brain to Sea Hawk

Milton was a little (a lot) disappointed that the path hadn't been made by wildcats or wild boars or wild anything, even though he had been a tiny bit nervous that they might eat him (sometimes Sea Hawk got eaten). Crouching down behind the broad sea grape leaves, binoculars to his eyes, he pondered his next move.

The thing was, being short, skinny, more than a smidge on the quirky side, and definitely not quiet, Milton hadn't always been the most popular kid in school. He still wasn't entirely sure how Dev, who was into tech stuff and video games, had become his best friend in third grade, when Milton had been firmly entrenched in his Nature Phase. He had though, and for three years the two had eaten lunch together and hung out after school, switching back and forth between building robots and birdwatching.

Then, last summer, Dev had attended Full STEM Ahead camp. Milton, bored and lonely, had started playing *Isle of Wild*. And when they started sixth grade at the big, new middle school, it felt like those two months apart had somehow overridden their last three years together. They weren't best friends anymore.

Then, after the Bird Brain Incident, they weren't friends at all. So, truth be told, Milton was less than thrilled by the sound of the boys' voices. Wildcats would have been far preferable. There was always a chance that they wouldn't have eaten him alive.

Milton was 99.99 percent sure that these kids would.

He started to back away slowly.

Then a voice yelled, "Hey, is someone down there?"

Egad! He'd been spotted.

Above Milton, two boys' faces had appeared at the railing of the tree ship. One was around his age and the other was maybe seven. They looked like brothers, with identical mops of curly dark hair and bronze skin. Their expressions, however, were not identical; the little boy's face was split in a huge, front-teeth-missing grin, while the older one's was scrunched up and closed.

Milton's first instinct was to yell *So long! Until we meet again!* and then bolt. He got as far as opening his mouth, when the older boy yelled down, "Who are you?"

And Milton had a revelation.

41

These boys didn't know anything about him. They didn't know about the Bird Brain Incident. They didn't know about his parents. They didn't even know his name.

He could be anyone.

Maybe they would invite him into their tree ship. Maybe they would help him fill his field journal. Maybe they would become friends.

Milton took a deep breath, smoothed his peacock feather, and called out, "Ahoy there! Permission to come aboard."

"Avast, ye scurvy dog!" the younger boy crowed down at him, still grinning.

"First answer the question," the older boy said, crossing his arms on the railing and peering down at Milton like a ship captain eyeballing a would-be stowaway. "Who are you?"

Who was he? Not Bird Brain, that was for sure. And not Milton P. Greene. No, if he could be anyone, Milton knew exactly who he would be, without a doubt.

"My name," he said, tipping his explorer hat, "is Sea Hawk. Sea Hawk P. Greene, Naturalist and Explorer Extraordinaire."

CHAPTER 12

From Sea Hawk to Bird Brain

In the tree ship, the older boy screwed up his face, and for a moment, Milton regretted his hasty self-renaming. *Isle of Wild* wasn't the most popular game, but it had a devoted fan base. What if these tree-shippers had heard of Sea Hawk?

He was relieved when the boy let out a *pshaw* and said, "I doubt it. What's your real name?"

"That is my real name," Milton said, trying to insert as much certitude as he could muster into his voice. "Sea Hawk P. Greene."

"Hey hey! I'm Gabe!" shouted the little boy, who was now shimmying up the ropes that served as the tree ship's rigging. "And that's Rafi! We're brothers, and our parents are entomologists, and we got here last fall, whatcha think about that?"

Milton shifted his smile to Gabe, who was clearly the more good-natured of the two. "I think I'm very pleased to meet you, Gabe," he said. "And antomologists." The word was vaguely familiar, but Milton couldn't quite place it. "So they know about . . . ants?" he guessed hopefully.

Rafi let out another noisy exhalation. "It's *en*tomologists," he said, "and they know about all kinds of insects. They *would be* studying the Incredible Symphonic Cicada here, except that stupid vine is in the way. Before this, we were in the Florida Keys for Schaus swallowtail butterfly research, and before that it was coffee berry borer beetles in Puerto Rico."

"A family of island-hopping scientists," Milton said admiringly (although he absolutely could not fathom why anyone would choose to study *bugs*). "How extraordinary!"

Rafi's face unscrunched slightly, but he didn't completely lose his captain-of-the-ship bearing. Milton wondered if he should offer some sort of tribute or perhaps kneel. He settled for taking off his hat and holding it over his heart. "Now that I've identified myself, may I please board your vessel?"

"Where'd you come from though?" Rafi asked, ignoring Milton's question.

"The Mariana Trench?" guessed Gabe, who was now hanging upside down from the topmost rope (Milton felt queasy even looking at him). "A volcano? Space? Another dimension?"

"I'm staying with my uncle, Dr. Evan Greene," Milton replied. "Maybe you know him?"

44

Rafi plucked one of the red banyan fruits from the branch next to him and lobbed it toward the palm trees beyond Milton. "There are like three people living on this island," he said. "Of course we know who he is."

Milton watched as the boy let another fruit fly. It didn't seem like a promising sign, those flying fruits. He was going to have to try harder.

"As it happens," Milton said, putting his hat back on, "I too am a scientist. I'm a naturalist. I, uh, I'm here doing a—a nature survey for the Flora & Fauna Federation." He pulled his field journal from his pocket and waved it around as proof. "Maybe you could help me? We could—we could do it together."

"I've never heard of the Flora & Fauna Federation," Rafi replied. "And I bet I know more about nature and biology stuff than you. I bet Gabe knows more than you."

"I do know a whole, whole lot," agreed Gabe, who was balancing on the railing like it was a tightrope (Milton had to avert his eyes). "And I'm a WordSmith! I'll help."

"Thank you, Gabe," Milton said. "I admit this is my first field expedition, but I can already tell that the Lone Island is a truly magnificent place. I'm sure you both agree."

"This island is maaagic!" Gabe sang out.

But Rafi was yanking even more fruit off the branch. This time he flung them at a tree that was much closer to Milton than he would have liked. "This island is definitely *not* magic," he said. "There are vines everywhere, there's hardly anything to do, and the only other kid sits in trees reading all day. We're leaving at the end of the summer, and I can't wait."

"You'll be pleased to know that I don't like tree-climbing or reading," Milton told him. "And I'm looking for a friend." He smiled his friendliest smile.

Rafi scowled, his lips pursed out like a grumpy duck. "Oh, goody," he said. "It's my lucky day. Dr. Bird Brain P. Greene has arrived."

Bird Brain. Milton actually stumbled forward, as if that great, invisible hand had followed him across the Atlantic just to give him another shove. "Oh, I'm not a doctor!" he said, too loud now. "Not yet anyway, although I do have quite a few areas of expertise."

"I don't need your expertise," Rafi replied, his voice louder too.

"My hope is to discover some brand-new species this summer, and with your assistance—"

"I'm not assisting anyone, Bird Brain," Rafi snapped.

Then he snatched up another very ripe, red fruit, and the force of the movement shook the tree limb so hard that a whole fruit shower came raining down.

Right onto Milton. One of them exploded on his explorer hat.

"So long, then!" Milton cried.

He turned and fled.

CHAPTER 13

The Restart

The trail that had led to the banyan continued, not farther into the island but parallel to the beach now. Milton hurried that way, picking seeds and squishy fruit pieces off his poor beautiful hat.

If he still felt like Sea Hawk at all, he felt like a mauled-to-death-by-rabid-fauna Sea Hawk. It was the Bird Brain Incident all over again, down to the avian moniker.

So long, Milton.

He wished he hadn't left the cottage. He wished he hadn't followed the trail. He wished he could hit *Restart*.

"Who needs friends? Who needs a super cool tree ship?" he said out loud as the path took him through a cluster of scarlet flower–covered trees. "If I can just find an outlet, then I'll have Sea Hawk, and Sea Hawk is all I need."

"Good thing," a voice said, "because that kook isn't into sharing the tree ship."

Milton spun around so fast that he stepped on his own feet and toppled to the ground. He stayed down, hands held up in the self-defense pose he had learned at his one-and-only karate lesson (martial arts were not really his thing).

"Who goes there?" he called, twisting left then right.

"Up here," the voice said.

Milton looked up. Perched in one of the flowered trees was a girl. She had large owlish eyes, deep brown skin, and a bun of dark hair on either side of her head. She was holding a book.

Here was Rafi's tree-climbing reader.

The urge to yell and run struck again, but Milton didn't do either. As mortifying as the last fifteen minutes had been, he realized that something extraordinary had just happened.

He had been brought back to life. This was a *Restart*.

"Are you Dr. Greene's nephew?" the girl asked. "He told my mother you were coming to visit."

Milton scrambled to his feet and held his hand up. "Indeed, I am!" he cried. "Greetings. The name's Sea Hawk. How do you do?"

The girl jumped down from the tree. Now that they were on level ground, Milton could see that she was much, much taller than he was. He also noticed that she was wearing a utility belt that was very similar to his own. Hers had a water bottle hanging from it and a little pouch into which she tucked her book (*Riveting and Remote: The Island of Fernando de Noronha* by Dr. Ada Paradis). She didn't shake his hand. Instead, she raised one eyebrow and asked, "Is that really your name? Didn't you just say something about Sea Hawk being all you need?"

"Oh! Did I?" Milton replied (very loudly). "That's right. Well. I was referring to . . . myself. All I need is me. Yes. I'm very . . . self-confident."

"So you're Sea Hawk?" the girl asked, eyebrow still up.

"Yes," Milton said. "That's me. Sea Hawk P. Greene. I don't know why everyone around here is so dubious about my name."

"Maybe because you don't seem like a Sea Hawk," the girl replied. "You strike me as more of a Grover or a Franklin or maybe a Percival."

"Despite my outward appearance," Milton said, "I have the heart of an adventurer. And my name *is* Sea Hawk. What's yours?"

"My name's Fig. Fig Morris." She crossed her arms, like she was ready to handle some name-dubiousity herself.

But Milton nodded enthusiastically. "Fig!" he said. "Fig. I really like that. You know some people think the fruit in the Garden of Eden was a fig?"

Fig relaxed her arms slightly. "Is that true? I didn't know that," she said. "Did you know that the banyan is actually a type of fig tree?"

"That's right!" Milton cried. "Sea Hawk's studied—I mean *I've* studied figs. *I* have." Fig's eyebrow was back up again. Milton rushed on, "So really *you* should be the captain of the banyan-tree ship. You're named after it."

"Maybe I should be," she replied with a shrug. "But Rafi would disagree. We don't exactly get along." She started to walk away from Milton. There wasn't a trail of any kind here, but she seemed to know where she was going. The sun shone through the leaves and lit up pieces of her as she went by, a patchwork of bright and dark on her khaki shorts and green T-shirt.

"Why not?" Milton asked, following her.

Fig glanced at him over her shoulder. "He made it very clear when he arrived that his family wouldn't be here long and that he wasn't interested in making friends," she said. She paused a moment, then added, "Also he called me Big Fig a few times, which I obviously did not appreciate."

"How heinous!" said Milton.

Fig waved her hand dismissively. "I don't care. He doesn't bother me. He's just intimidated by me."

"Because you're tall?" Milton asked, walking double time now so that they were side by side. "I've often wished I was tall. As a species, humans are getting taller, so evidently natural selection favors the vertically superior. I'm due for a growth spurt any day now, so I *could* catch up to you, but I highly doubt it. Plus, you might have another growth spurt too. I wonder what height you'll—"

"Seriously, Sea Hawk?" Fig cut him off, coming to a sudden stop. "I like the way I look, but that doesn't mean I want to have a conversation about it with you."

If Milton was tall, he was pretty sure he would like nothing more than to converse about his tallness. But it was clear that for Fig, this was Things You Do Not Say territory.

"Got it, Fig," he replied quickly. "Whatever you say, Fig."

Maybe it was because his HandHeld was dead and *Isle of Wild* was out of reach. Maybe it was because things had gone so terribly wrong at the tree ship. Maybe it was because she wore a utility belt (like him) and seemed fearless (unlike him). Maybe it was because he had spent the last year or maybe even longer feeling loneliness like a dull, constant ache that started in his (very sensitive) stomach and spread over his entire body, from the tips of his cowlicky brown hair to the ends of his poorly tended toenails.

Milton wasn't sure exactly why. But he was sure of this:

More than anything in the world, he wanted Fig to be his friend.

He wasn't going to mess up this *Restart*.

CHAPTER 14

The Youngest Naturalist in the World

When Fig started walking again, Milton went along with her. She glanced quickly at him, then sped up, but Milton sped up too. Together, they speed-walked out of the cover of the trees and toward the beach, at the far north end of the bay. The rocks were bigger here, towering above their heads, and there was a carpet of beach sunflowers beneath their feet.

Milton was breathless almost immediately from trying to keep up with Fig's long strides, but he managed to pant out, "So, Fig, how long have you lived here?"

"Almost two years," she replied, not one bit breathless. "My mother's in charge of the Truth-Will-Out Vine study."

"So she works with my uncle!" Milton cried. "I bet they're friends."

Fig shot him a tiny smile and slowed down a tad. "They actually are," she said.

Milton grinned. "I knew it," he said. "And you—" He paused to choose his words carefully. "You like the Lone Island?"

"I don't always love *living* on an island in the middle of nowhere," Fig told him. "But I do love this island. It's—I think it's a special place. I wish I could have met Dr. Paradis though. She traveled everywhere on her sailboat, exploring and researching. But once she found the Lone Island, she stayed put." She shrugged. "I guess she thought it was a special place too, even if it is covered in vines. Anyway, she's one of my mother's heroes. That's why she took this spot when Dr. Greene offered it to her. Well . . . that's one of the reasons."

Fig fell silent as they reached the sand, and Milton paused to yank off his hiking boots (nothing worse than sand-filled footwear). Up beyond the dunes were the cottages, and Milton could see Uncle Evan, who was carrying an enormous cardboard box, and two other scientists coming from the direction of the docks.

"Those are Rafi and Gabe's parents, Dr. Alvarez and Dr. Alvarez," Fig said, pointing to the couple who was approaching the cottage covered in the heart-firefly-fairy mural. Dr. Alvarez had curly dark hair like his sons, while Dr. Alvarez had a long braid and wore a flowing, flowery skirt. Both of them were smiling ear to ear as they talked animatedly to each other.

"That is . . . not what I expected Rafi's house to look like," Milton said. "Or his parents."

Fig laughed. "They're into connecting with the earth and that kind of thing. They're sort of like hippies. Hippies who are crazy about bugs."

"I don't think they passed their earth-loving ways to their son," Milton said. "Or their cheerful dispositions."

Fig laughed again, and Milton patted himself on his back. Things may have started off a bit shaky, but Fig's mother was friends with his uncle, and Fig loved the island, and after two laughs in a row, he figured it was the perfect time to share the details of his new, sure-to-amaze identity.

"You may be interested to know," he said, "that I too am in the natural sciences. I'm conducting a nature survey for the Flora & Fauna Federation this summer." He pointed to the badge on his vest with three green *F*s arranged in a pyramid (which he had custom-ordered online for one low payment of $25.99 plus shipping). "We call it the Triple F."

"The Triple F, huh?" Fig said. "They employ nine-year-olds?"

"Nine-year-olds!" Milton was aghast. "I'm not nine. I'll be thirteen in eight months!"

"Oh, sorry," Fig said. "You're just . . ." She paused, then shrugged. "Anyway, twelve is still a little young to be employed, don't you think?"

"Oh, it is," Milton agreed. "I'm probably the youngest naturalist in the world." He pulled out his field journal, flipping it open to the

Nature Sightings Checklist in the back, right to the page with the (extremely impressive) *Komodo dragon* check mark. "See? I already got started on the survey."

Fig barely glanced at the journal. "Sure, Sea Hawk," she said. "Listen, this is my house, so I'm going to head in, and you should too. The mosquitoes will be coming out soon and believe me, you don't want to be out here when they do."

Milton pulled his waterproof watch from his utility belt. "Would you look at that!" he cried. "It's almost six o'clock. Can you believe I've been on the trail for hours?"

Fig didn't answer. She was already halfway up the dune, heading toward the cottage with the yellow door that Milton had chickened out of scouring for electrical outlets that morning.

Electrical outlets. The HandHeld! That was what he'd set out to do—find an outlet—and he'd never even brought it up.

"Fig! Wait!" Milton shouted after her. "Does your home happen to have electricity?"

"No," Fig called back without even turning around. "There isn't any over here."

It was somewhat expected but still devastating news. There wasn't time to dwell on that right now though. Fig was getting away. "How about we meet up tomorrow?" he cried. "You can go exploring with me."

55

"No, thanks. I've lived here for two years, remember? I don't need a tour guide."

"Oh, I know that! What I meant was that *you* can show *me* around. I'll even let you name one of the new species we find."

Milton heard Fig make a noise halfway between a sigh and a laugh, but she still didn't turn around.

He couldn't let his *Restart* end this quickly. He racked his explorer hat–covered brain for something that would convince her to hang out with him again. "I'll give you partial credit when I submit my nature survey to the Triple F. And—and it'll be an adventure!"

Fig paused.

Then her sunshine door opened, and a tall woman with a head-wrap that made her even taller appeared. "Hey, Figgy," Milton heard her say. "Did you spend any time with your feet on the ground today?" Then she noticed Milton. "Well, who's this?"

"That's Sea Hawk," Fig told her mother.

"Hello, ma'am," Milton said from the bottom of the dunes. "I was just trying to persuade your daughter to accompany me on a scientific expedition tomorrow."

"Isn't that nice," Fig's mother replied, beaming down at him.

Then Fig's mother looked at Fig, her eyebrow arched. Fig looked back at her mother, her eyebrow arched. They seemed to be passing some sort of secret eyebrow-code message. Milton held his breath and waited.

Until finally, Fig's mother nodded, and Fig sighed and called back, "Fine, Sea Hawk. Meet me at the docks at seven a.m."

Milton pumped his fist in the air as Dr. Morris waved goodbye and Fig shut the door behind them.

This Sea Hawk thing was actually working!

CHAPTER 15

Following the Milton Macaw

Milton left his encounter with Fig and her mother feeling like that great, invisible hand was now giving him little pats on the head. Those totally, terribly, horribly, heinously rotten thoughts were nowhere in sight. He'd spent the year with Sea Hawk as his only friend, and now, less than twenty-four hours after arriving on the Lone Island, he had become Sea Hawk and he'd made a friend.

Well, maybe a friend.

He was almost back to Uncle Evan's when he spotted what he thought might be another trail branching off the pebbly road. It was even less worn than the banyan trail, only a slight indentation in the dune grass. It made Milton wonder if a family of scurrying opossums might have gone that way, or maybe a flock of high-stepping spoonbills.

He hesitated for a moment, thinking of the late hour and Fig's warning about the mosquitoes.

But then he remembered who he was now.

He was Sea Hawk.

Sea Hawk wouldn't go home. Sea Hawk would go onward, ever onward.

So—chest puffed out, fruit-stained explorer hat set at a jaunty angle—onward Milton went.

After hiking through the dune grass for quite a while, he came to a place where the trees grew taller than any he had seen on the island yet. It was peaceful there, in the shade of those towering trees, with the smell of flowers in the air and birds singing overhead.

And then, in the middle of the tall trees, there was a clearing.

And in the middle of the clearing, there was a house.

Not a thatched-roof cottage, but a two-story, wood-framed, tin-roofed house. It was old and weathered-looking, with peeling yellow paint and a sagging white porch. Sun-faded hibiscus-print curtains were drawn over the windows, and railroad vine had crept over the front path as if no one had gone in or come out in a long time.

Milton knew, of course, that this must have been the home of the once-very-famous and now very-much-deceased Dr. Ada Paradis.

It didn't look like a place that should be disturbed, this abandoned home on the edge of the jungle, but Milton tiptoed forward anyway, peering every which way through his neon-green binoculars. He saw some fascinating ferns by the front door, a nest in one of the oaks, and a few orange-and-purple butterflies.

He was just thinking that he would definitely come back tomorrow with Fig for further observations when he saw something move.

Something very fast. Something teal. Something flying through the air, soaring between palm fronds, toward the back of the house.

"Great flapping falcons!" Milton cried, hurrying after the flash of color. "What could that be? Maybe some sort of tropical bird. Maybe a never-before-seen tropical bird. I'll call it the Lone Island Parrot. No—the Milton Macaw!"

But when he rounded the house, there was nothing there.

Nothing but the vine wall.

Milton thoroughly searched the area with his binoculars, but try as he might, he couldn't find any sign of the bird.

"What did you do with that magnificent specimen?" he said to the vines. He noticed that unlike ordinary vines that were rooted in the ground, these vines somehow swung freely, like the wooden-bead curtain in Uncle Evan's cottage. He tried to see what was behind them, but no matter how many strands of green he pushed aside, there were always more. "I say, cough up the Milton Macaw!"

As if in response, the vine in his hand rustled.

60

Milton knew it was the wind (islands in the middle of the ocean tend to be very windy). But he kept talking to the vine anyway.

"I know the Milton Macaw is in there," he said. "And who knows how many other never-before-seen animals you've got in your vicious green grasp."

The vine loomed above him, and Milton suddenly had a truly horrifying thought: What if this super-fast-growing vine could grow right over him? He threw aside the strand he was holding as he imagined the vine creeping up around his ankles, wrapping around his legs, getting tighter and tighter, eventually covering him completely, leaving him invisible and silent and alone forever.

But now, as the wind blew (it was blowing, wasn't it?), the vine's bright green leaves seemed to wave at Milton. They didn't look particularly scary, waving hello like that. They didn't look like they would swallow him whole and mummify him. They looked like friendly leaves.

"Perhaps you're not all-the-way awful," Milton allowed. "Maybe you can't help growing over the whole island and ruining everything you touch."

Up close, he now saw that the vine was quite pretty, so startling green and covered in teeny-tiny white flower buds. He started to feel kind of bad about how he had considered machete-ing them down earlier. Apologetically, he ran a finger down one of the strands, then held it in his hand, letting the greenness twine around his wrist.

"I'll let you in on a secret, Truth-Will-Out Vine," he said. The buds seemed to open the slightest bit. The leaves waved. The unfelt wind seemed to blow harder. "I haven't always been Sea Hawk P. Greene, Naturalist and Explorer Extraordinaire. My name is actually Milton—although most people have been calling me Bird Brain lately. Or nothing. And before I was Sea Hawk, I used to ruin things all the time too."

Milton gave the leaves a commiserative pat.

And then the vine did something very unexpected.

CHAPTER 16

Behind the Vines

The vine in Milton's hand began to shiver. It began to wriggle.

Then it ripped itself out of his grasp and spun upward, like yarn being rolled into a ball. The vines on either side did the same, wrapping themselves up and up.

Milton leaped backward, let out a caw, and assumed his self-defense pose, but the vines took no notice. They kept spinning, five, ten, fifteen feet up into the air, until they stopped.

The vines hung there, quivering balls of green, waiting.

Milton stared up at them, hands still ready to ward off blows, mouth still agape in shock. Then he looked down below them.

And there it was.

On the ground, there was a small, muddy, green metal box. Milton hadn't noticed it before because until the vines had rolled up, it had been completely hidden beneath them.

He glanced hesitantly up at the vine-balls once more before kneeling down to examine the box. There was no lock on it, only two simple latches. He started to flip one open.

It was then that the first mosquito landed on Milton's nose.

The mosquito was the size of a hummingbird, and its big, bulgy red eyes were excessively creepy up close.

Milton screamed. He smacked his face so hard that the bug burst, its insides splattering across the lenses of his glasses. As he tried to wipe enough guts off so that he could see, he felt something land on his ankle.

Then something landed on his elbow.

Then his pinkie finger.

Then his other elbow.

The mosquitoes were attacking!

Milton grabbed the green box, jumped to his feet, and took off. As he ran, he could hear the buzzing of the mosquitoes zipping by his ears. It was very unnerving, so he started screaming again to drown out the sound.

When he reached Uncle Evan's cottage, he threw himself through the front door. Uncle Evan must have heard him coming (not surprising given the volume and high pitch of Milton's vocalizations), because he was waiting with the most heavy-duty, industrial-size flyswatter Milton had ever seen. As soon as Milton slammed the door shut, Uncle Evan started swatting. Smooshed mosquito carcasses fell left and right.

"All clear," Uncle Evan said, after the last insect had exploded in a gory detonation of blood and guts and wings. Uncle Evan didn't seem fazed by the carnage. He gestured to the driftwood table, where two bowls were waiting. "Come tell me about your day before our spaghetti and meatballs gets any colder."

CHAPTER 17

Prodected and Fwee

Under ordinary circumstances, Milton wasn't known for his secret-keeping ability. He was known, in fact, for his blurt-everything-out-immediately tendencies.

These, however, were not ordinary circumstances.

Something decidedly *extraordinary* had happened behind Dr. Paradis's house, and Milton felt sure that the only appropriate response was to do something extraordinary himself. The problem was, he had no idea *what* had happened or what he should do. He definitely needed some time to figure it all out.

So he plopped onto a stool and said loudly, "If you're wondering about this box here, it's not mine. It's Fig's. She let me borrow it after a long day of expeditioning in the great outdoors."

Milton had never been a very good liar, but Uncle Evan seemed so pleased that he didn't even notice how unnaturally high Milton's voice was and how wide and unblinking his eyes were.

"You spent the whole day exploring and you made a friend, Milton?" he asked.

"I go by Sea Hawk now," Milton informed him. "But yes, I did. At least, I think I did. We're going to explore some more tomorrow too."

Uncle Evan smiled a slightly-wider-than-smallest smile across the table. "That's really great, Mil—I mean, Sea Hawk," he said. "How about the day after that you and I go for a hike? I can—I should take a morning off. I should try to enjoy the island every once in a while."

"Okay, but first, I need to ask you something very important," Milton said. "Where can I charge my HandHeld? I searched your entire cottage this morning, and there are no outlets."

Uncle Evan gestured to the oil lamp and then to the camp stove. "I thought you knew," he said. "There's no electricity over here."

Milton lowered his head to the table with a *thunk*. "How do you live?" he groaned. Then he lifted his head slightly. "Perhaps we can search for the Milton Macaw on our hike," he said. "That's a new species I found today."

"There's nothing I'd like more," replied Uncle Evan.

After dinner, Uncle Evan sat at the table and sorted through the paper-filled cardboard box he had brought back from the research

67

station. Milton peered over his shoulder for a while, reading snippets of the field reports and research papers the Lone Island scientists had produced over the years. When he got bored, Uncle Evan gave him a copy of Dr. Paradis's *Glacial and Glorious: The Desolation Islands* to peruse. Milton wished there were a few more pictures and a few less words, but all in all, it wasn't the worst way to pass the time until his uncle said good night and went through the beaded curtain.

Only when the cottage-shaking snores started did Milton bring the green metal box onto the pull-out couch.

He'd assumed the latches would be rusted shut or at least a little jammed. He'd imagined using pliers or a wrench or whatever kind of tools people used for hard-to-open things. But the latches lifted easily, and when he pulled the lid up, there was a suctiony sound that told him the box had been airtight.

Inside was a thin pile of pages. Milton thought these pages were paper, but on closer inspection, he found that they were actually some sort of large, cream-colored leaf. The leaf-pages were bound together with pieces of Truth-Will-Out Vine, and there were words on them written in black ink.

Carefully, he lifted the stack of leaf-pages from the box, and in the flickering light of the lamp, he whisper-read the first one:

The Adridged Lone Island Field Guide
By Dr. Ada Paradis

Milton clutched his vest-covered heart. "I say," he breathed. "What a discovery."

He adjusted his glasses, took a deep breath, and turned to the next page:

Dear Guide Finder,

If you arr reading tis, I am dead, and the magnifycent island I have loved and comserved for fifty years is in terrible janger.

Put feer not! Somewhere in the jumgle, I have left vou a treesure that will keep the Lone Islard prodected and fwee. To find this treasure, yoo will have to follow dhe clues along the way and wittin the pagez of this field guide. If you succeed, yuu will have broved yourself to the island and truly earnud the treasure and all it entails.

So off you go, Guide Finder, on a wild and wondrous adventure. The Lone Island awaits!

Simcerely,
Dr. Ada Paradis

CHAPTER 18

Never-Before-Seen

Milton sat on the couch-bed gawking at the letter he'd just read (slowly because of all the weird misspellings). Then he read through it again (even more slowly). Then, struck with a burst of egad-can-you-believe-thisness, he threw the field guide into the air.

It came fluttering down like a many-winged Milton Macaw and landed open on a page with a pen-and-ink illustration and a block of carefully printed text. The illustration showed a cluster of vines with friendly leaves and tiny white blossoms. Seeing those vines was like seeing a familiar face, and Milton eagerly read the entry:

Truth-Will-Out Vine

Where else could you start but at the Truth-Will-Out Vine? This epiphytic plant may be the most misunderstood of the Lone Island flora.

Not a destroyer but a protector, the vine's unique survival adaptation is the island's first line of defense. It has stood firm (or hung firm, rather!) against many would-be Lone Islanders with questionable intentions over the years. If you want to find the treasure, you will first have to go back and decode the truth about the Truth-Will-Out Vine. Then go forward and tell your own, which, if you have found this guide, you have already begun to do.

Habitat: Forms a dense perimeter around the island's interior

Population Estimate: Millions and millions of strands

Disposition: Perhaps a tad overcautious, but always willing to listen to those who have nothing to hide

Not so familiar after all. Neither Uncle Evan nor Fig had mentioned any of this about protectors and truths. And what did Dr. Paradis mean about the vine listening? Hat-topped brain buzzing, vest-covered heart pounding, Milton flipped to the next leaf-page.

There he found an illustration of a big-eyed, long-winged bug with another name he recognized: Incredible Symphonic Cicada.

These were the bugs that Uncle Evan had mentioned in his letter, the ones that Rafi said his parents were having a hard time studying because their habitat was in the vine.

Now Milton was turning leaves rapidly. He saw illustrations of a mouse-like creature with a spiraled nose, of some kind of tentacley water monster, of huge umbrella-shaped flowers. There were entries with titles like *Tone-Deaf Warbler* and *Yes-No-Maybe-So Tree* and *UnderCover Cat*.

And there were also these: a pachyderm that lived underground, a tree that shot poison arrows, and a bird with stars in its tail feathers.

"These are the never-before-seen creatures!" Milton whisper-yelled into the silence of the cottage, springing from the couch-bed.

Field guide clutched in his hand, he started toward the beaded curtain, ready to leap onto Uncle Evan's bed and holler *See here! I have found Dr. Paradis's guide to the flora and fauna you seek!* It would be a truly grand moment. Uncle Evan would probably cry with happiness.

But then, out of the corner of his eye, Milton spotted Sea Hawk in the kitchen.

He swung around to face the peacock-feather-hatted, explorer-outfitted figure and found himself eyeball to eyeball with—

Himself.

It was his blurry reflection in the icebox.

"I'm Sea Hawk," Milton said aloud. "Naturalist and Explorer Extraordinaire."

What would Sea Hawk do if he found a guide to hidden treasure inside a mysterious box underneath some bizarro spinning vines?

The answer was the same as it had been earlier at the trail: Sea Hawk would go onward, ever onward.

Staring at himself now, Milton decided that if he was really and truly going to be Sea Hawk P. Greene, then that was what he would have to do.

He would follow the clues (whatever they were). He would find the treasure (wherever it was). He would save the island (from who-knew-what kind of danger). He couldn't play *Isle of Wild* right now, but he could live it.

Then he could really amaze Uncle Evan, and Fig would be thrilled to work on a nature survey with him, and Rafi would invite him into the tree ship.

And maybe his parents would come to the island to see his brilliance in action. Maybe Dev would hear about it. Maybe everyone at school would. Or even everyone in the world. No one would ever call him Bird Brain ever again.

Yes, indeed, suddenly and unexpectedly, things were looking up for the boy formerly known as Milton P. Greene.

Before he went to sleep, Milton pulled out his field journal and wrote his first-ever entry. Then he set the alarm on his waterproof watch, took off his glasses, and turned the oil-lamp wick down until the flame went out.

It still took him a while to fall asleep, true. But it wasn't because he was thinking about totally, terribly, horribly, heinously rotten things or even *Isle of Wild*.

Milton lay awake in the silence and stillness of the night, and he thought about what he'd written in his field journal:

This may turn out to be the Most Seriously, Supremely, Unexpectedly, Astonishingly Spectaculous Summer of All Time!

74

CHAPTER 19

The Biggest Ecological
Discovery of the Century

The next day, Milton woke up at 5:30 a.m. He did not want to be late for his meeting with Fig. She didn't seem like she would stand around and wait for him.

Uncle Evan was still asleep, his snores so loud they vibrated the bead curtain as Milton pulled on his explorer gear. He tucked his journal and Dr. Paradis's field guide into one of his zip-up pockets, then checked the silver icebox for breakfast possibilities.

Only leftover spaghetti and meatballs.

He decided to pass on breakfast.

Fig wasn't at the docks when Milton arrived there at 6:02. She wasn't there at 6:17 or 6:33 or 6:49 either. When Milton finally saw her walking down the beach, he checked his watch. It said 6:58.

And when Fig set her foot down on the weathered planks of the dock, the watch read 7:00 exactly.

"Want a banana?" she asked, holding one out to him.

"Do I ever!" Milton cried. "I was beginning to think spaghetti and meatballs was the national dish of the Lone Island."

Fig raised her eyebrow at him. "Spaghetti and meatballs? Why would you think that?"

Milton didn't answer on account of the stuffed-full-of-banana state of his mouth.

"Anyway, let's get going," Fig said. "There's a lot I can show you. Usually remote islands have hardly any plants or animals, but the Lone Island is full of wildlife—at least the parts not covered in Truth-Will-Out Vine are."

"You don't know the half of it," Milton said, pressing his hand to the field guide in his pocket.

Fig led him to the south side of the docks. When the same kind of crab Milton had seen yesterday scurried across the rocks, Fig told him its Latin name (*Johngarthia lagostoma*), which Milton thought was extremely impressive. So impressive that he wondered if she might have at least a little information about the wildlife in Dr. Paradis's field guide. However, when he asked, "Do you suppose a hundred-legged cephalopod might eat one of those for lunch?" her response was: "I have no idea what you're talking about."

Next, she led him to the nests of several bird species, like the brown noddy and the phoenix petrel, but she seemed flummoxed when he asked, "Have you ever heard a birdcall that might possibly be described as, I don't know, tone-deaf?"

She showed him tracks on the main beach where green sea-turtle hatchlings had skittered into the ocean that morning, but didn't even bother to respond when Milton wondered aloud, "I wonder what sort of tracks an invisible feline might make."

By the end of this very physically active morning, Milton was more worn out than he had ever been, and when Fig suggested that they take a break, he collapsed onto the ground in the middle of the beach path. Fig walked over to the shade of a rain tree (Latin name *Samanea saman*) and took a book out of her utility-belt pouch.

"I say, this explorer stuff is hard work," Milton said, crawling over to her. "I'm having a splendid time, of course." He leaned against the tree and stretched out his aching legs. "The only thing that would make it more splendid would be an outlet and a little time with Sea Hawk."

Fig peered over her book at him. "A little time with whom?"

Not again. "With myself!" Milton shouted.

Fig pulled her head back. "Seriously, Sea Hawk, why are you yelling?" she asked. "And why do you keep talking about yourself like that—*Sea Hawk* this and *Sea Hawk* that? And why are you so obsessed with electricity?"

"I'm not yelling!" Milton yelled. "And I'm not obsessed. Everyone likes electricity. For vacuum cleaners and air conditioners and—and video games."

Fig's eyes narrowed now. "Video games? So, what, have you been hoping I'll lead you to a secret electrical outlet this whole time so you can stop hanging out with me?"

"What? No! I would never devise such a dastardly plan!" Milton cried.

"You know, I never said I was looking for a friend," Fig said, tucking her book back into her pouch and starting to rise to her feet. "I was fine being by myself."

"No, I know! *I* wanted to be *your* friend. I still want to. Wait—don't go!" Milton pressed his hat to his head. His thoughts slipped and scrambled, struggling to find purchase, to find a way to keep his *Restart* from ending so soon.

There was only one thing for it.

"Oh, Fig, I just remembered," he said, jumping to his feet. "I found something you're going to love. Want to see it?"

He didn't wait for her answer. He unzipped his pocket and yanked out Dr. Paradis's field guide. The leaf-pages crinkled and fluttered as he thrust them toward Fig, a please-still-be-my-friend smile on his face.

Hesitantly, Fig took the pages.

She read the first one.

Then she looked back up at him with her mouth hanging open, her owlish eyes even bigger and rounder, and all thoughts of electricity obsession and third-person referencing obviously gone.

"Sea Hawk," she said, "this might be the biggest ecological discovery of the century."

CHAPTER 20

Sea Hawk and Fig: Naturalists and Explorers Extraordinaire

Field guide in hand, Fig led Milton to her cottage. Her mother was at the research station, so they had the place to themselves.

Even though the cottage looked exactly like Uncle Evan's from the outside (except for the sunshine door), the inside was another story altogether. The Morris house was cozy and bright. There were comfy rugs on the floors, bookshelves full of books and knick-knacks, sea-glass wind chimes in the windows, and two colorful, swirly paintings on the walls.

"My dad painted those," Fig said, when she saw Milton squinting at them.

"He's good," Milton replied, although he didn't know much about art. He had tried to illustrate his field notes a few times during his Nature Phase, but everything he drew looked like an amoeba on toothpick legs. "Very good."

"He was very good," Fig said quietly.

Milton spun away from the paintings. "Fig, I didn't—you never said—" He felt like he had one foot in Things You Do Not Say territory and the other in Things You Should Absolutely Say (But Maybe Don't Know Exactly How To) territory.

Fig shook her head and took a seat on the cushy red couch. "Never mind, Sea Hawk," she said firmly. "It happened a long time ago, and it doesn't bother me. Let's talk about this." She held up the guide.

"Whatever you say, Fig," Milton said, hurrying to plop down beside her.

Fig set the guide between the two of them and turned to the page after Dr. Paradis's letter, which was a table of contents. It read:

Then Fig moved on to the entries, one after another. Milton tried to read along, but she read a lot faster than he did.

When she reached the end of the final entry, the Yes-No-Maybe-So Tree, Fig stared at the illustration of the paper-and-pen-covered tree for a long time. Then she cried, "But this is ridiculous!"

"I think you mean *spectaculous*," Milton corrected.

Fig shook her head. "We already know about the Truth-Will-Out Vine and the Incredible Symphonic Cicada, but the rest of these—they can't possibly be real."

"Why not?" protested Milton, who had never once considered this possibility. "Think of all the magnificent creatures in nature—lizards that walk on water, chimps that know sign language, goats that climb up practically vertical cliff faces."

"That may be true," Fig half allowed. "I once read that we've only discovered twenty percent of Earth's species so far. Way less if you count bacteria. But even if these creatures do exist, what's all this about treasure and protecting the island?"

"I don't know what the danger is exactly," Milton said, "or what the treasure could be, but I think the field guide is like an actual *guide*. If we follow the clues in it, we'll find whatever it is Dr. Paradis wants us to find."

Fig turned the guide's pages slowly again, pausing here and there. "I guess I see some clues. Dr. Paradis mentions canoeing here in the *Push-Pull Centopus* entry . . . and camping under a Starlight Starbright Tree on the *Astari Night Avis* page . . . and listen to this: *Yes, Little SmooshieFace knows it all.*" She tapped on these words under the image of the pointy-eared, bushy-tailed Beautimous Lemallaby. "Does that mean we're supposed to ask this flower-bootied lemur-wallaby for help? And then what? It's going to answer?" She flipped back to the beginning of the guide with a shrug.

Milton gasped as a vision of a miniature green-eyed bobcat meowing in a language only Sea Hawk could understand came to him. How had he not realized this before? "Little SmooshieFace shall be my Dear Lady DeeDee," he whispered.

Luckily, Fig didn't hear him. She had half jumped to her feet and was now sinking back down, the guide in her hands opened to the *Truth-Will-Out Vine* entry.

"Sea Hawk, listen to this," she said. "*Where else could you start but at the Truth-Will-Out Vine?* The path to the treasure must *start* at the vine!"

"Brilliant!" Milton cried. "It makes sense too. I found the guide beneath the vine behind Dr. Paradis's house. And I only saw it because the vines rolled themselves up."

Fig tipped her head in confusion. "Well, the vine is an epiphyte," she said slowly. "It doesn't have roots, so it blows around easily. That's probably what happened." She went back to Dr. Paradis's letter, running her fingers over each line. "The misspelled words have to be clues too, right?"

Milton knew that Sea Hawk took diligent, detailed notes. He knew that Fig could probably spend the rest of the day reading the field guide over and over (up in a tree, no doubt), and that really was probably the wisest course of action.

But Milton was not interested in the wisest course of action right now. His sensitive stomach was flipping over and over like someone was cooking pancakes in his belly. Chocolate-chip-and-awesomeness pancakes. "Perhaps," he told Fig. "Probably. There are lots of clues, right? And we can figure out all of them along the way. Let's go find some treasure!"

Milton was sure Fig would protest. He was pleasantly surprised when instead she said, "All right, let's do it," with the start of a smile.

He bounced on the couch in excitement. "Yes!" he yelled. "Sea Hawk and Fig, Naturalists and Explorers Extraordinaire!"

Fig didn't cheer along with him. Her smile had disappeared already.

"Sea Hawk," she said.

Milton kept bouncing. And yelling.

"Sea Hawk!"

Milton shut his mouth. But he kept bouncing.

"You know we have to show this to your uncle and my mother, right? And the Drs. Alvarez?"

Milton stopped bouncing.

"Absolutely," he said. "Eventually. After we find the treasure, right?"

Fig crossed her arms and frowned at him.

"My uncle actually knows about some of these creatures already," Milton told her hastily. "He told me about them forever ago."

"I guess that does make a difference," Fig said. "But studying the Lone Island is literally my mother's job. And this island—covered in that vine and with the hidden cicadas—it's almost like it doesn't want to be studied. My mother always says the island is worth getting to know, no matter how long it takes, but she also says your uncle has been getting more and more discouraged with their research."

Milton thought of his uncle—his tiny smiles and his sad eyes that reminded Milton of his own father's this past year. He hadn't been like that when he'd visited seven years ago; seven years ago, Uncle Evan had been brimming with energy, overflowing with stories, certain that he was about to find the creatures in this very field guide and more. "Mighty moles and voles." Milton sighed. "You're right. We'll show them. But let's try to do *something* ourselves first. I'd like—I'd like to have an adventure for once."

Fig studied him for a moment. "I might be ready for one too," she said finally.

If Fig had really wanted to show the field guide to Uncle Evan and her mother right then, Milton knew they would be heading to the research station, no matter what he said.

But they didn't.

They went back outside and headed toward the Truth-Will-Out Vine, ready to start.

CHAPTER 21

Living on Vine Time

Milton and Fig spent the afternoon together. Walking the perimeter of the vine wall, they pulled aside strands and searched for any gaps in the growth. They checked the vine beginning at the docks and ending near the tree ship before deciding to call it a day.

Milton had planned to continue treasure-hunting the next morning, but instead he woke up to an alarm going off and then his uncle, disheveled and bleary, came stumbling through the bead curtain.

"Ready for a hike?" he asked Milton.

"Am I ever," Milton said, hopping up and pulling on his vest and hat. It was early enough that there would still be plenty of time for treasure-hunting after.

Uncle Evan led Milton off the pebbly path to a part of the island he hadn't seen yet, farther beyond the docks than he had gone with Fig. They squelched down maze-like paths between mangroves, sidestepping roots that were like hundreds of fingers reaching out of the sludgy mud. They stood side by side and tracked the flight of a wandering albatross, binoculars up to their eyes. Milton asked a thousand questions about the flora and fauna around them, and Uncle Evan patiently answered each and every one.

It was impossible for Milton not to think about the weekend expeditions he'd gone on with his parents as he and his uncle explored the Lone Island together, but he tried his best not to. There was too much rottenness tied up with those thoughts, and he wanted to just be here right now.

Two hours later, they arrived at Dr. Paradis's house, entering the clearing on the south side.

"This is where I saw the Milton Macaw," Milton told Uncle Evan, leading him around to the back of the house. "It was teal and very fast."

"I think I might have actually seen your bird before," Uncle Evan said, squinting at the house under the brim of his (not nearly as awesome as Milton's) hat. "Sometimes I come over here when I need to think. When Dr. Paradis was alive, this was her favorite spot. We had a lot of great conversations here."

"Standing here? I would have figured a great explorer like Dr. Paradis would always be hiking around, searching for wildlife," Milton said.

Uncle Evan shook his head. "Her health was already poor when

I arrived," he said. "This was as close to the jungle as she could get, and she loved to watch the vines blowing in the wind. She would stand right here by them and tell me, 'Evan, the Lone Island awaits! When will you be ready to go out to meet it?'"

The Lone Island awaits! Milton recognized those words from Dr. Paradis's letter. And the place that Uncle Evan was pointing at— it was exactly where Milton had found the field-guide box! What if, Milton thought, Dr. Paradis had wanted Uncle Evan to find the guide?

"Anyway, I know *you've* been going out to meet the island," Uncle Evan continued, putting a hand on his nephew's shoulder. "I know that's what your parents hoped you'd do. And I haven't enjoyed the Lone Island like this in years." He gave Milton one of his small smiles. "Thanks, Sea Hawk."

"Anytime, Uncle Evan," Milton told him as he promised himself that once he figured out at least the first clue, he would tell his uncle everything.

And then Uncle Evan would really smile.

Later on, Milton met up with Fig again. In fact, every day that week Milton met up with Fig to search the vines. While they were at it, they searched for the rest of the field guide's flora and fauna too.

"Obviously it wouldn't be as good as finding the treasure," Fig said. "But I'm sure my mother and the other scientists would be thrilled to have proof that any one of these creatures is real."

So they checked every tree trunk for the holes that could possibly launch poison thorns. They listened to every bird's song, then argued over whether it sounded horrendous enough to come from a Tone-Deaf Warbler. They waded as far upstream as they could in the thin, trickling river that emptied into the ocean, but the Truth-Will-Out Vine blocked their way before any hundred-legged centopuses came into view. They even dug holes in the sandy soil, hoping to uncover one of the sure-to-be massive tunnels of the EarthWorm Pachyderm.

Milton's days were full and active and, frankly, completely exhausting. Out in the sun with the earth under his feet, he started to feel the way he used to in his Nature Phase—like he was more alive, more himself, but in a good way, in the best way possible.

But sometimes at night, when his hiking boots were kicked off and the wick on the lamp was turned down and Uncle Evan was snoring away, Milton's rotten thoughts still showed up. In those moments, with nothing else to fill the silence or distract his mind, Milton reminded himself that he wasn't Bird Brain anymore. He wasn't even Milton anymore.

He was Sea Hawk, and he was on a quest for treasure.

CHAPTER 22

Dr. Bird Brain & Big Fig

On Milton's eighth day on the island, he and Fig went down to the rocky north end of the bay to take another look at the river basin. Upstream, the wall of Truth-Will-Out Vine extended across the river, but before that, there was a long stretch of vine-free jungle.

"These trees are some of the tallest I've seen on the island," Fig told Milton as they stood on the riverbank, surveying the area. "I'm going to climb up for an aerial view."

"I will be remaining on solid ground," Milton replied. "But may I suggest that peely, sunburny-looking tree right next to the vine wall over there?"

"That's a gumbo-limbo," Fig said, following his point. She tucked the field guide into her book pouch. "Latin name *Bursera simaruba.* And it's perfect."

They took off their shoes and squished through the sandy mud toward the scaly red-trunked tree. Little silver fish darted away from them with every step, their scales flashing like tiny bolts of underwater lightning.

"Do you think these are the Itty Bitty Fish, Fig?" Milton called, pausing so that the shiny, tiny fish would float closer. "The ones the guide says the Push-Pull Centopus eats?"

"What's a *centopus*?" asked a voice behind them. "What are you doing in the mud? Can I come in the mud? I'm coming in the mud."

Milton jumped and turned to see Gabe splashing toward them, a gap-toothed grin on his face. Behind him, motionless on the riverbank, was Rafi. He had a camera around his neck, one of those old-fashioned, box-shaped ones.

Instantly, Milton felt queasy. He and Fig had never talked about it, but they had both been avoiding the tree ship during their island explorations.

"Are you doing the nature survey right now, Sea Hawk?" Gabe asked. "We're doing one too!"

"Ah," Milton replied. "I see. Well. How nice."

He glanced warily downriver again, but Rafi hadn't moved except to hold up his camera.

"Ours is going to be way better," Rafi called. "It's going to have photos."

On his face was that captain-of-the-ship expression. Milton didn't reply, because he was 99.99 percent sure that whatever he said would be wrong. He was relieved when Fig, who was staring fixedly ahead, said loudly, "Sorry, Gabe, but Sea Hawk and I can't talk right now. We're very busy searching for something that will save the island."

"Oooh," said Gabe, who was now lying on his stomach in the shallow water. "Save it from what? Dinosaurs? Pirates? Rising sea levels?"

"From nothing," Rafi said after a *pshaw*. "They're making it up, Gabe."

"We're not," Fig replied. She started toward the gumbo-limbo tree again. "Come on, Sea Hawk. Let's continue our search over by the vines."

"Right you are," Milton said, wading after her as fast as he could.

Gabe, dragging himself through the water, shouted, "Is that what you're searching for? Vines? There's a bunch down there. And there. And there too. I can help!"

"Gabe!" Rafi yelled. "Come back. You're doing a survey with me, remember? You're not here to help Dr. Bird Brain and Big Fig with their Triple Fake make-believe."

Fig stopped trudging forward so abruptly that Milton almost fell over, even though he was ten feet behind. It was like a shock wave had rolled off her, and when she spun around, both her eyebrows were at Maximum Arch Capacity.

"For your information," she snapped, "we're following clues that Dr. Paradis left in a secret field guide."

"Fig!" Milton cried. Then he saw that she was unzipping her book pouch. "Come to your senses, my good woman! It's not for their eyes."

But Fig, it seemed, was not interested in being sensible. She pulled out the crinkly leaf-pages and stomped through the water toward Rafi, who hastily scrambled farther up the riverbank.

"The clues lead to a treasure," Fig said, holding up the guide. "A treasure that will protect the island."

"*X* marks the spot, me mateys!" Gabe cried. "Yo ho ho!"

Rafi inched toward Fig, looking definitely confused and very wary but more-than-a-little curious. "No way," he said. "That's a bunch of leaves you two scribbled on."

Milton hurried over to Fig and took the guide from her. "You're not supposed to tell anyone yet," he whispered.

Rafi was right in front of them now. He reached out and touched the thin, veined pages of the guide. He seemed awestruck by its awesomeness. While Milton would absolutely not have chosen to spill their secret plans at this early stage, he couldn't help but feel proud that he was in possession of something that Rafi was in awe of. He thought Rafi might possibly be at least slightly in awe of him now too.

Then Rafi snatched the guide.

Well, he tried to. Fig's hand was there first, and the guide was back in her pouch before Milton even realized he wasn't holding it anymore.

"I just want to look at it!" Rafi protested, his face going grumpy duck–like. "Anyway, I bet I could tell you all kinds of things about the island that you don't know."

"I doubt that," Fig replied.

"Fig knows the Latin names of trees," Milton told him as bravely as possible. "And, as I've told you, I work for the Flora & Fauna Federation."

Rafi scowled. "Even if I believed you, that doesn't mean you should keep the guide for yourselves."

"We could help!" Gabe said from the river, where he was now making kissy faces at the maybe–Itty Bitty Fish that surrounded him.

Fig shook her head. "Sorry, but no," she said. She tilted her head toward Rafi. "You've been very rude to Sea Hawk, calling him names. And to me, but what else is new. *And* you hate this island."

"That's true," Gabe agreed.

"No, it's not!" Rafi cried. "I mean, it's not the whole truth. I don't *hate* the island. I just don't want to live here. And I never—you were the one—it's not like you've ever been that nice to me."

Fig didn't answer. She swung around and splish-sploshed her way back toward the gumbo-limbo.

Milton certainly wasn't going to be left behind with Rafi. He high-tailed it after her without so much as a *So long.*

CHAPTER 23

Truly Missing Out

Rafi and Gabe didn't stick around for long, but even after they were gone, Milton couldn't seem to regain his adventuring mood. He felt flustery and fumbley, and his thoughts weren't exactly sunshine and rainbows after being *Bird-Brain*ed yet again.

Fig definitely wasn't in the adventuring mood either. Over an hour later, she still wasn't talking much and she wasn't smiling at all. Milton had tried to make jokes (including this gem: *What did the UnderCover Cat say to the marine biologist? Don't study me— I'm not a SEE creature!* Get it?). He'd let her sit in the tree in silence for ten whole seconds. He'd read aloud from the *Lemallaby* entry, which was his favorite, but to no effect.

It didn't help that she couldn't see anything beyond the Truth-Will-Out Vine except more Truth-Will-Out Vine (not even with Milton's binoculars).

"You and Rafi really don't like each other, do you?" he finally said as Fig gave up and started climbing down the gumbo-limbo.

"Can we not talk about that kook?" Fig said, scooching her way down a limb. "I don't care about him. He doesn't bother me."

It wasn't the first time Milton had heard Fig say this, and it wasn't the first time he didn't exactly believe her.

"But that's not one hundred percent true, is it?" he pressed. "You showed him the field guide—the *secret* field guide—so you must care a little."

He stood by the vines, watching as Fig expertly placed her feet into tiny crevices he couldn't even see and lowered herself to another limb. There was a long pause before she said, "I guess I wanted to show him that he was missing out."

"He is. He is indeed," Milton said. He smoothed his peacock feather, then picked a few of the tiny Truth-Will-Out flowers, trying to find the best words for what he wanted to say next. Then he gave up on *best* and blurted out, "I would also like to thank you for defending me so admirably!"

Fig jumped down in front of him. "You mean telling Rafi he can't call you names?" she said. "You don't have to thank me. Any friend would do that."

But that, Milton knew, also wasn't true. And the way he'd found that out featured prominently in his nightly rotten thoughts.

After the Bird Brain Incident, Milton had been suspended for three days (unjustly, he believed). On the morning he returned to school, he went to his locker to get his books. Dev's locker was a few feet away, but he wasn't there yet.

Then a group of boys—older boys that he didn't even know—spotted him from down the hall. "Hey, Bird Brain!" one of them yelled. "Welcome back!"

It didn't take long for the boys, cawing and laughing, to surround Milton, and it didn't take long for other kids to crowd around to watch.

Milton's sensitive stomach had done 360s as he stood pressed against his locker, surveying the taunting faces in front of him. He had been teased before, he had been picked on before, but he had never been truly afraid before. He was afraid then, and when the first boy pushed him, he started searching for someone, anyone, who would help him.

Then he'd spotted someone. He'd spotted Dev. His best friend was there, standing by his locker, gripping his backpack straps, watching with big eyes. But he didn't say a word.

And neither did Milton. No one would have heard him over the cawing anyway. Instead, he put his head down and shoved past the boys, running straight to the bathroom. Safe in the stall, he closed the toilet lid, hopped up, and got out his HandHeld (which his mother had thankfully forgotten about that morning). He became Sea Hawk for a while.

No one would dare make fun of Sea Hawk. Milton was sure of that.

"Not any friend," he told Fig, his eyes on the vine he was now wrapping around his hands. "And if I may say, anyone who can live on this island for a year and not spend time with you is *truly* missing out."

Fig smiled at him. "Well, anyone who doesn't invite you into their tree ship is missing out too, Sea Hawk," she said.

Milton's insides went all warm and a little mooshy. It felt nice, but just thinking about how nice it felt made the feeling start to go away. He was still opening and closing his mouth, trying to think of keep-the-feeling words, when there was a whooshing sound and suddenly, his hands were empty.

CHAPTER 24

Proof in the Pickle

The sound was like a strong breeze blowing through the vines, transforming them into flora wind chimes. The strands that had been in Milton's hands had yanked themselves away, joining the Truth-Will-Out Vine wall.

"It's happening again!" Milton gasped.

Fig gasped too as she backed away from the writhing, wriggling mass of greenery. Then the vines rolled up exactly as they had behind Dr. Paradis's house. But it wasn't a box that these vines had been hiding.

It was a tree.

The tree was even taller than the gumbo-limbo, but much thinner, with a black-green trunk. It didn't appear to have bark but was instead sort of shiny-waxy and covered in even blacker-green knots, like the skin of a toad. The branches had a few heart-shaped leaves here and there.

The real focal point of the tree, however, were the fruits that hung by the hundreds up and down the branches: oblong, olive green, and very puckery-looking.

"Is that the Sweet Pickle Tree?" Fig exclaimed. "The one the Incredible Symphonic Cicadas like?"

"I don't see how it could possibly be anything else," Milton said, sniffing the suddenly brine-pungent air.

Then there was another sound. Not a whooshing, not vine chimes, but a sort of rustling, clicking, shifting sound. A sound like teeny-tiny claws scraping and teeny-tiny legs skittering and teeny-tiny holes opening.

All around the Sweet Pickle Tree, the ground started to move.

Something was wriggling its way to the surface. Well, *somethings*. Hundreds of somethings actually.

Hundreds of bugs.

Each bug was about the size of an unnervingly large cockroach. Their bodies were shiny black, and their eyeballs and wings were white, and they were crawling out of the ground at an alarming rate.

Fig's eyes were as huge as Milton had ever seen them. "It's the Incredible Symphonic Cicadas," she said. "They're emerging."

"I wish they wouldn't," Milton said with a shudder. "They do this every summer?"

"Yes, they live underground for most of the year, then come out to reproduce," Fig said. "This is the third emerging my mother and I have been here for, but we've never actually *seen* the cicadas. They feed on the Truth-Will-Out Vine sap, remember? So they're always hidden behind layers and layers of it. The Alvarezes have only been able to get their hands on two specimens."

Even more of the black-and-white bugs were surfacing now, skittering over one another, swarming upward like they were in some kind of insect marathon and the gold medal was at the top of the Sweet Pickle Tree.

"This. Is. Gross," Milton groaned, one hand on his stomach and one over his mouth. "Really gross. I might puke."

"We've got to catch one," Fig said. "We need all the proof we can get!"

Then there was yet another strange noise.

This time the noise came not from upward-burrowing or tree-climbing, but from contracting muscles and buckling membranes. The sound, like a violin string being plucked, was followed by more of the same, coming from random places on the tree. It seemed to Milton like the bugs were preparing to do something, and he was 99.99 percent sure he was not going to like whatever it was.

The sounds continued, here, then there, here, then there, and then suddenly—everywhere.

Not only from the Sweet Pickle Tree but from all over the interior of the island, where other cicadas must have been emerging.

The noise was clearly made by insects; it had that scratchy, whiny, buggy sound. But somehow it was also . . . a song.

There was melody, high and sweet. There was harmony, low and slow. There were sudden interjections like percussion and moments where only one insect could be heard—a solo. The music swelled and expanded and intensified into an insectival crescendo as Milton listened.

"This is super beautiful," he whispered to Fig (gross bugs or not, he didn't want to interrupt a performance like this).

But Fig was busy unzipping a pocket on her utility belt. From inside, she produced a small plastic jar with a hole-poked lid.

She held it up for Milton to see and gave a nod that he assumed was supposed to be meaningful.

Then Fig dove for the Sweet Pickle Tree.

The music of the nearby cicadas faltered for a moment, but quickly got back on track. Fig, muddy-kneed and grinning, held up her container triumphantly.

There was a long, green, puckery fruit inside.

And latched on to it was a tuxedo-wearing Incredible Symphonic Cicada.

The proof was in the pickle.

CHAPTER 25

A Bug in a Jar Is Worth Two in the Vine

Bug in jar in hand, Fig ran toward the cottages, and Milton hurried after her. By the time they reached her sunshine door, the droning of mosquitoes had begun.

"Here you two are!" called Dr. Morris as they burst inside and slammed the door. She was in the kitchen area, stirring something in a big pot. "You want to stay and eat, Sea Hawk? I don't know if you like paella but—"

"Yes!" Milton yelled. "Yes, yes, yes. Anything but spaghetti and meatballs."

Dr. Morris laughed. "Did you know your uncle brings that for lunch every day? He doesn't even stop working to eat it either. You should tell him he's welcome to come by for dinner and a night off of worrying about this island sometime."

"I'm sure he would be very pleased to be invited," Milton said.

He and Fig sat on the comfy red couch. Because Dr. Morris was only about ten feet away, they held a whispered debate.

"Should we tell my mother now?" Fig glanced over her shoulder at Dr. Morris, who was getting plates down from a curtained shelf. "She'd be so happy."

"Uncle Evan would be happy too," Milton whispered back. "But now that we found the cicadas, I feel like we're this close"—he held up his finger pinched almost to his thumb—"to getting the treasure."

Fig nodded. "You were right about the vines," she said. "Somehow, they can move, and we have to figure out *how*." She very slowly unzipped the pouch that held the cicada jar and peered in. "Did you know that cicadas can't actually eat things? Their mouths are like straws, so this one is just sucking the juice out of that fruit right now. See?"

Milton did not see, because he was looking anywhere but at the jar in the pouch. "Does the grossness never end?" he said with a shudder. "But it *is* a pretty juicy pickle, so the cicada should be able to survive, right?"

Fig nodded. "For at least a day or two, I think. We can go back to the Sweet Pickle Tree tomorrow. And I'm going to get started on the spelling clues too."

"Dinner's ready," Dr. Morris said from right behind them.

"AHHH!" Milton screamed while Fig hastily rezipped the pouch.

"What are you two whispering about over here?" Dr. Morris asked.

"Oh, nothing!" Milton cried. "Nothing at all! And may I say, Dr. Morris, that your cooking smells truly heavenly. I can't wait to eat it and talk exclusively about its deliciousness and—"

"It's a surprise, Mama," Fig said in a normal-volume voice. "We'll tell you in a few days."

CHAPTER 26

Last-Chance Chats

By the time Milton left the Morris house, it was late enough that the mosquitoes had dispersed. "They're crepuscular," Fig had assured him before he walked through the sunshine door. "So they mostly feed at dawn and dusk."

Milton highly respected Fig's opinion on scientific matters, but he still ran as fast as he possibly could down the beach road and up to Uncle Evan's front porch.

Uncle Evan was apparently of the same mind as Fig because he was there on the porch, perched on a camping chair, gazing out to sea with no heavy-duty flyswatter in sight.

"Missed you at dinner," he said, patting the chair next to him.

"I was at Fig's," Milton said. He sank down as the now-familiar, end-of-the-day tiredness spread through him. "Dr. Morris said you should come over sometime."

"I know I should," Uncle Evan replied with a sigh. "I haven't been over to the Morrises' or the Alvarezes' in months. I haven't sat outside like this in a long time either."

He resumed his ocean-gazing. The wind was calmer than usual, and the waves were gentler, their breaking a whisper rather than a shout. With no artificial lights to interfere, thousands and millions and billions of stars were visible, both above and reflected in the surface of the sea.

It was incredibly stunning, and Milton understood that his uncle was basking in the beauty and serenity and that he should keep quiet. "Let's have ten seconds of silence" was something his mother was fond of saying. So he started to count to ten.

He made it to six.

"I say, Uncle Evan," he began, trying not to sound overly interested, "did you happen to hear those Incredible Symphonic Cicadas?"

"I did," Uncle Evan said. "Aren't they something?"

"They are . . . something," Milton replied, suppressing a shudder. "But hearing them got me thinking—you told me you hadn't found any never-before-seen creatures, but that's not entirely true. The Truth-Will-Out Vine and the cicadas are brand-new species, aren't they?"

"You're right about that," Uncle Evan said, nodding without taking his eyes from the starry night. "But I didn't find them myself. When I was in grad school, I wrote Dr. Paradis dozens of letters begging her to let me do research here. I thought this island was my chance to do something great . . . and to be some*one* great. When she finally said yes nine years ago and I showed up here, the vine and the cicadas were the first things she showed me."

"She *told* you about the other wildlife though, right?" Milton pressed. "The pachyderm that lives underground and the tree that shoots poison arrows and the bird with stars in its tail feathers?"

Uncle Evan shifted in his chair, like he wasn't quite comfortable. "She did. She said that she'd found hundreds of species and that there were hundreds more out there, but I'd have to find them myself. And, well, as you know, I never have."

"But they're here, aren't they?" Milton asked, gripping the arms of his chair. "Don't you think they're somewhere on the island?"

"I don't know anymore, Sea Hawk. I've been working and researching and trying—" Uncle Evan turned toward Milton and found a pair of bespectacled eyes a few inches from his face (so much for looking not-too-interested).

"Dr. Paradis wouldn't have made them up!" Milton cried, still very close to his uncle.

Uncle Evan scooted his lawn chair back a few inches and considered his intense-faced nephew. "No, I don't think she made them up," he said. "Dr. Paradis was known to be a brilliant, eccentric person, but not a liar. But I've—if I haven't found those creatures by now, I don't think I ever will."

Uncle Evan sagged into his chair, and Milton felt a tad guilty. He had wanted more information, but instead he'd reminded his uncle yet again of how he'd failed. The way his uncle was sitting there reminded Milton so much of his father that it made his heart squeeze and his stomach ache to look at him.

"Uncle Evan, why did you mention the cicadas to my father?" he asked. "In your letter. You said they'd be coming out soon, and this might be his last chance to hear them."

Uncle Evan straightened up. "So your dad spent some time on the Lone Island once," he said. "Maybe he didn't mention it? It was a few years ago. He'd been asking and asking me to come visit again, but I wasn't . . . I wasn't making any progress here on the island, and I didn't want to leave. So finally, he came here."

Milton pressed his explorer hat to his head. "My father? On the Lone Island? He barely even likes the great outdoors!"

Uncle Evan laughed his out-of-practice, choky laugh. "Maybe not now, but when he was younger, your dad and I were always outside. In fact, by the end of the visit, he was even talking about getting a degree in biology and moving you all here."

"Great flapping falcons!" Milton said. "We could've become Lone Islanders? Why didn't we?" He paused. "And why didn't he bring me?"

"I think he needed some time on his own, time to figure a few things out," Uncle Evan said slowly. "Even back then, he and your

110

mom weren't doing so great. She was working more, and he was unhappy with his job, and they weren't—I don't know, it's hard to say what went wrong, especially from thousands of miles away. He had the idea that moving here would fix things, give everyone a chance to sort of start over."

"Like a *Restart*," Milton said.

"Yeah, like that," Uncle Evan agreed. "But then he realized that bringing you all halfway around the world to live on a remote island might not be the most realistic plan." He shrugged one shoulder. "As for this being his last chance to hear the cicadas, well, I wrote that because I was worried the Lone Island was going to be sold, and it looks like I was right."

CHAPTER 27

Something Truly Spectaculous

Milton was so surprised, he sprung out of his chair and would have fallen right off the porch (a deadly eighteen-inch plummet!) had Uncle Evan not caught his arm. "Sold?" he cried. "To whom? *By* whom?"

"That's a bit tricky to explain," Uncle Evan said, guiding Milton back to his seat. "There's a very old, weird law that says the United States will back any claim a citizen makes on an uninhabited island as long as there's seabird poop there."

"Bird poop? Are you making this up, Uncle Evan?"

"I'm not," Uncle Evan said. "Bird poop isn't exactly valuable these days, but the law still stands and because of it, Dr. Paradis owned this island. It was hers, and she could have left it to whoever she wanted when she died. But she didn't leave a will behind, and she has no living relatives."

Milton scooched his chair closer to his uncle. "So who owns the island now?" he asked.

"No one," Uncle Evan replied. "Which means the future of the island has been in the hands of the courts. It's such a complicated case that it's been up in the air since Dr. Paradis's death. I've been petitioning the entire time to have the island designated as a protected wildlife refuge, but there are other interested parties who have been requesting permission to buy the island." He paused, wearily running a hand over his face. "The courts contacted me a few weeks ago to say they were getting ready to make a decision on the island's future soon and that if I had any last research findings, now was the time to submit them. So that's what I've been doing pretty much nonstop. That's why I've been so busy."

"But you don't think it'll work?" Milton asked. "You don't think they'll listen to you?"

Uncle Evan shrugged. "Six years ago, I was sure I would have found enough new species to convince anyone in the world to protect this island, but that hasn't happened yet. If I can't get the courts to give me more time, then they'll likely allow the government to sell the island to one of those other interested parties, probably the Culebra Company."

"Who are those scoundrels?" Milton demanded. "A rival research society?"

Uncle Evan shook his head. "No. It's a real estate development group, and one with an abysmal environmental record no less."

"But—they can't—what will they do to—egad!" Milton sputtered.

Then he remembered what he had. Well, actually, what Fig had right now. "What if I could give you some of Dr. Paradis's notes about the plants and animals she said were here?" he shouted, leaping to his feet again. "Or what if you had an Incredible Symphonic Cicada?"

Uncle Evan had sunk back into his chair. It looked like he had sprung a leak, like he was folding up on himself. "I know Dr. Paradis took extensive field notes—hundreds of pages. She showed me some of them once, but I couldn't find them when she died. Without physical proof of the species though, the notes have very little value. As for the cicada, we've been able to get a few specimens over the years, and they are fascinating, but even a cicada wouldn't help now. The Culebra Company has invested a lot of money and time and lawyers in trying to get this island, Sea Hawk. The courts are almost certain to side with them."

Now Milton felt as leak-sprung and deflated as Uncle Evan. He plopped not onto the chair, but onto the boards of the porch. His peacock-feather-hatted head was hung low. Here he had thought this was the Most Seriously, Supremely, Unexpectedly, Astonishingly Spectaculous Summer of All Time, only to find out that he was

114

wrong, wrong, wrong. It was still the Most Totally, Terribly, Horribly, Heinously Rotten Year of All Time. He was 100 percent sure of it.

"It would take something truly spectacular to save the Lone Island now," Uncle Evan said quietly.

Save the Lone Island—mighty moles and voles! The words launched Milton to his feet. That was what he'd been trying to do ever since he found the field guide! The only thing that had changed was that now he knew what the danger was.

The treasure was still out there.

And the boy formerly known as Milton P. Greene was going to find it. He was going to be bold. He was going to be brave. He was going to be awesome.

He wasn't going to give up on the Lone Island.

"If something truly spectaculous is what you need," Milton declared, one finger raised to the sky, "then something truly spectaculous is what I shall find."

Uncle Evan watched his nephew with such a jumbly mishmash of an expression that Milton couldn't really tell what he was thinking. "I hope you do," he said. "Now I think it's time for bed, Milton."

"My good man, I go by Sea Hawk now," Milton reminded him.

"Oh, that's right," Uncle Evan said. "I think it's time for bed, Sea Hawk."

CHAPTER 28

Every Second of Every Day

Just like that, the treasure hunt had turned into something super important with very high stakes. The island was officially in danger (serious danger!), and Sea Hawk and Fig, Naturalists and Explorers Extraordinaire, were the only ones who could save it.

As soon as the sun came up the next morning, Milton raced to Fig's sunshine door.

Dr. Morris, eyes half-closed and bathrobe on, opened it. "Good morning, Sea Hawk," she said. "To what do we owe the honor of this entirely too early visit?"

"Good morning," Milton said, panting. "Is Fig home? It's an emergency!"

"Like a true emergency?" Dr. Morris asked, her eyebrow arching, Fig-like.

"Like a Sea Hawk and Fig, Naturalists and Explorers Extraordinaire, emergency. Something terrible is going to happen to the Lone Island!"

Dr. Morris smiled sadly. "You must have heard about the upcoming court decision."

"Mama told me last night," Fig said, coming out onto the porch holding two oranges. "Let's get to work."

"Fig says you have a plan to save the island," Dr. Morris said, giving her daughter and her peacock-feather-hatted friend a fond smile. "If anyone can, it's you two."

After Dr. Morris returned inside, Fig handed Milton one of the oranges and began marching around to the back of her cottage. There was a yellow-flowered paradise tree (Latin name *Simarouba glauca*) on the edge of the jungle there. It was Fig's favorite spot, and once she went up, Milton knew it would be very hard to get her down.

"We need to solve these clues fast," she said.

"Agreed," Milton said. "Let's go back to the Sweet Pickle Tree and check out that moving vine." He walked at a slight diagonal in hopes of herding Fig away from the tree, but Fig was very un-sheeplike. She did not adjust her course, so he ended up smooshing into her.

She cast him a sideways glance and shrugged herself away. "Sea Hawk, quit walking kooky," she said. "We need to get serious. That was a big breakthrough yesterday, but if we're going to figure out this vine thing, we can't keep ignoring the other clues."

"I have no idea what you're talking about," Milton replied as Fig

117

reached the tree and boosted herself up. "I've been extremely serious this entire time."

"The misspelled words, Sea Hawk," Fig said. She pulled the field guide out of her pouch and handed it down to Milton, open to the vine entry. "Look, the guide practically tells us they're a clue. *If you want to find the treasure, you will first have to go back and decode the truth about the Truth-Will-Out Vine.*" She leaned over to tap the line insistently. "*Go back and decode*, Sea Hawk. That means there's a clue before this entry. And what's before the entry? The letter!"

Fig had brought up the misspelled words when they found the guide and a couple times since, but she'd never insisted that they focus on them before. Milton had a hunch that she'd been enjoying hiking around the island as much as he had. But now, up in her perch, Fig flipped open her notebook, ready to work.

"Have you considered that maybe Dr. Paradis simply wasn't the best speller?" Milton said. "Many geniuses aren't, like Albert Einstein for example."

"I made a list last night," Fig said, ignoring him. "I think this is all of them."

She held up her notebook so that Milton could see the page. It read:

1. adridged
2. arr

3. tis

4. magnifycent

5. comserved

6. janger

7. put

8. feer

9. jumgle

10. vou

11. treesure

12. islard

13. prodected

14. fwee

15. yoo

16. dhe

17. wittin

18. pagez

19. yuu

20. broved

21. earnud

22. simcerely

"That looks like a very nice list," Milton said. "Perhaps you can contemplate it as we stroll over to the Sweet Pickle Tree."

"Perhaps not," Fig replied. "I think this is important, so this is what I'm going to do today. You don't have to help me though. We don't have to be together every second of every day."

Milton felt the words pierce his vest-covered heart.

"But we're friends," he said.

"That's true." Fig was studying her list intently. "We can do our own thing sometimes though."

Milton stood beneath Fig, gripping the field guide and feeling suddenly seasick and small. He'd felt this way plenty of times before, most recently when Rafi had shaken banyan fruit onto his magnificent headwear.

But this was worse. So much worse. Because this was Fig.

Fig saying *So long.*

"Fine," Milton said, shoving the field guide into one of his zippered pockets. "That's fine. But I'm off to find a way through the vines. I'm off to save the island. I'm going onward. *By myself*!"

Fig was staring at him, but Milton didn't wait for her to reply. He ran toward the river, a lone Naturalist and Explorer Extraordinaire.

CHAPTER 29

A Lonely Day on the Lone Island

It was a long, lonely day for Milton. He wandered along the river-banks, but the Sweet Pickle Tree had vanished behind the vine again. He dug around in the dirt trying to find some more cicadas, but came up empty-handed (he didn't really want to find those super gross bugs anyway). He had to eat cold spaghetti and meat-balls for lunch. Again.

The worst part was listening to the words Fig had said replaying over and over in his mind: *We don't have to be together every second of every day.*

It wasn't the first time Milton had heard that.

From third through fifth grade, Milton and Dev had sat together at lunch every day. In the beginning of sixth grade, they had still sat together, but Dev had started doing things like shushing Milton when he spoke too loud or asking if he could talk about something *other* than *Isle of Wild*, but then not really listening when Milton did. Then one day, while they were waiting in the lunch line, Dev had suddenly blurted out, "I'm going to sit with some other friends of mine today, Milt."

"Oh," Milton had said. "I see. Other friends. What other friends?"

"Some kids I met over the summer," Dev had said. "At Full STEM Ahead camp. You don't know them."

"I don't," Milton had replied. "But *we're* friends. You should sit with me."

Dev had gotten a little angry, which he almost never had before, and he'd snapped, "It's one lunch, Milton. We don't have to be together every second of every day."

Which had eventually meant that they weren't together very many seconds of almost any day.

Then, after the Bird Brain Incident, not ever.

If it had meant that then, how did Milton know it didn't mean that now?

And, of course, Dev hadn't been the only one to leave that year.

Yes, it was a rough day. A day of the great, invisible hand flicking him in the back of the head. A day of totally, terribly, horribly, heinously rotten thoughts. For the first time since he'd found Dr. Paradis's guide, Milton missed *Isle of Wild*. He missed it suddenly and completely, deep in his sensitive stomach. He missed Sea Hawk's booming catchphrases. He missed Dear Lady DeeDee's meowing chitchat. He missed turning off parts of his mind and falling into the story.

He knew he was supposed to be Sea Hawk in real life now, and that had actually been going shockingly well. But he didn't feel like Sea Hawk today. He didn't even feel like Milton P. Greene. He felt like Bird Brain.

It was a terrible feeling.

Milton was sitting by the edge of the river, watching the Itty Bitty Fish (if that's what they were) swirling around in the water and rereading the field-guide entries when a hand reached over his shoulder and tapped the illustration of the EarthWorm Pachyderm.

"What's that supposed to be?" demanded a voice.

"AHHH!" Milton screamed. He flipped the guide shut and jumped to his feet.

Rafi, box camera around his neck, started and stumbled back. "Whoa, relax," he said. "I just asked what that thing was. Can I look at it?"

"What? Hmm. I'm—I'm not sure," Milton stammered. "I mean, perhaps not." Then, remembering how Fig had defended him so boldly (back when they were friends), he straightened his glasses, smoothed his peacock feather, and said, with as much Sea Hawkian bravery as he could muster, "No, you may not."

"Why?" Rafi asked, fingers fiddling with his camera buttons. "I could help." Which surprised Milton until he added, "You two probably don't even know what you're doing. Right, Gabe?"

Gabe didn't answer, but Milton could hear him belting out a wordless song somewhere nearby.

"I told you, I'm—I'm employed by the Flora & Fauna Federation," Milton said. "And Fig and I have already made several very significant discoveries. We've practically found the treasure."

Rafi scowled his grumpy-duck scowl. Then, before Milton even realized what was happening (his reaction times not being the most tiptop), Rafi snatched the field guide right out of his hands.

"I say, you—you scoundrel!" Milton cried. He took a deep breath, then made a grab for the guide. "Return it immediately!"

"Let me look for a second," Rafi said, holding the leaf-pages out of Milton's reach. "*Really-Sharp-Schnozzed Shrew.* No way." He continued reading aloud, while Milton continued trying to retrieve the guide. "*The Really-Sharp-Schnozzed Shrew and the EarthWorm Pachyderm are not overly fond of each other and have been known to have 'nose-offs,' where each attempts to murder the other using only its honker as a weapon.* Is this a joke?"

"It is not," Milton replied.

"This can't be real," Rafi said, shaking his head. "Gabe, come over here and listen to this!"

No one answered.

"Gabe!" Rafi hollered. He folded (mangled!) the field guide, tucked it into his pocket, and took a few steps in the direction of the vines. "Gabe?"

Still no one answered.

Then there was a scream.

CHAPTER 30

The Nose-Off

Truth be told, what Milton wanted to do was run far, far away from the screaming. He 100 percent did not want to do what he did (and later would sort of marvel at himself for doing), which was take off running after Rafi.

The boys raced through the jungle, past the palms and ferns and mangroves that grew near the river. The vine wall was ahead of them, swaying gently in the breeze, but Gabe was nowhere in sight.

Then there was another yell, and Milton saw that right in front of the vine, the ground had collapsed.

Gabe was at the bottom of a hole.

Rafi swung his camera around to his back and hurried to kneel at the edge (much closer than Milton would deem safe). "Gabe!" he called. "Are you in there? Are you okay?"

"Hey hey," came Gabe's voice, high and shaky and muffley-echoey. "Think so. Hit my head."

Milton crept a few feet closer until he could peer into the pit. It was deep, maybe ten feet or so, and there was a lot of dust, but he could see Gabe down there, sitting cross-legged on the sandy ground with quite a lot of blood coming from a cut on his forehead.

Milton did not like blood. He never had. If he saw even a little bit (like a paper-cut amount), he would feel queasy. The more blood there was, the queasier he got. He backed away from the hole.

"I have to get him out of there," Rafi said, jumping to his feet. He grabbed a nearby palm frond only to toss it down right away (not strong enough). He snatched up a fallen mahogany-tree limb, then dropped that too (not long enough).

Milton tried to think of something useful to do—something useful that didn't involve looking at Gabe's gross, bloody head—while Rafi raced around frantically. There was silence from the hole.

Then there was a tiny, barely audible squeak.

"I say, are you quite all right in there, Gabe?" Milton called.

"Monster," came a super, super soft whisper. "Big ol' scary-lookin' monster."

Rafi cast an alarmed glance at Milton, and they both rushed to the edge again.

127

There was Gabe, huddled up against the far side of the hole. Now that the dust had settled, Milton could see that the hole extended out underground, so that it was really the end of a tunnel.

And in that tunnel, only about a room-length away from Gabe, was an absolutely enormous and completely bizarro creature.

The parts of the creature that were not covered in mud were pinkish and slime-shiny. It appeared to have no eyes, no legs, no real distinguishing features at all, except for a large snout. The snout was like an elephant's trunk, except that it was the same slick pink as the rest of its body, and instead of having nostrils at the end, there were rows of gray, square, rocklike teeth.

Teeth that were mashing and crashing and grinding against one another.

The creature was waving its enormous honker in a manner that appeared very menacing from Milton's point of view (he could only assume that Gabe felt the same way). It had to be—

"The EarthWorm Pachyderm!" Milton shouted.

"The what?" Rafi cried. "What's that? And what's it doing?"

At first, the only thing Milton could remember from the *Earth-Worm Pachyderm* entry was that it ate dirt. That meant it wasn't a carnivore. It was huge and weird, but it shouldn't want to attack Gabe.

Then he remembered the *Really-Sharp-Schnozzed Shrew* entry that Rafi had sneered at down by the river.

"The pachyderm must think Gabe's a Really-Sharp-Schnozzed Shrew," Milton said slowly. "Both animals dig holes, and both are territorial. It's challenging him. This is a nose-off!"

Rafi gaped at him, and Milton could see that he was remembering the words he'd read aloud too—especially the part that said *each attempts to murder the other.*

"We need to get Gabe out now," Milton said. "That thing's going to eat his nose off with its nose!"

Rafi darted back to the discarded palm frond. Milton (briefly) considered running away again. But he couldn't. He couldn't yell *So long!* and bolt no matter how scared (and grossed out) he was, not with Gabe in danger. If ever there was a time for him to show—to prove—that he was indeed Sea Hawk P. Greene, that time was now. And, in fact, Milton realized, Sea Hawk himself had been in a very similar situation once.

Sea Hawk had been traipsing through the jungle when the ground had given way beneath him, plunging him into the den of an extraordinarily fierce and unusually immense honey badger. It hadn't been a super difficult adventure. Milton had simply made Sea Hawk duck, twist, and emit his signature bird-of-prey call while removing rope from his utility belt, tossing it around a boulder at the top of the hole, and then scrambling up to safety.

Gabe didn't have a rope. Milton didn't have a rope. But he did have—

"The vines!" he shouted.

He hurried over to the mahogany tree and started unwinding the first vine he came to as fast as he could. Rafi understood right away and came to help. When they had a pretty long strand free, they tossed it into the hole.

The end of the vine landed next to Gabe, and he grabbed on—

But his sudden movement made the EarthWorm Pachyderm advance! It wriggled toward Gabe, closer and closer, its nose swinging faster than ever.

"Don't move, Gabe," Rafi instructed.

Milton's brilliant idea hadn't been enough. His Sea Hawkian confidence began to wane. And Gabe had such a tiny little schnoz. He didn't stand a chance!

"I wish Fig was here," he groaned. "I don't know if I can do this without her."

In his hands, the Truth-Will-Out Vine twitched. Then it jerked upward, pulling Gabe toward the surface a few feet. Down in the hole, the EarthWorm Pachyderm paused.

"What's happening?" Rafi cried. "What did you do?"

"Nothing," Milton replied, shaking his head.

"Well, do nothing again, Dr. Bird Brain!" Rafi shouted.

Bird Brain. It was really such a stupid nickname. It wasn't clever or even terribly mean. Even so, hearing it made Milton feel like he'd just gotten another smack from the great, invisible hand.

But something about those words—or maybe that smack—jarred an idea loose in his head.

Most people have been calling me Bird Brain lately, he'd told the vines the day he had found the field guide, the day they had rolled up like enormous balls of green yarn. The ins and outs of exactly what that meant weren't clear in Milton's mind, but he followed his (sensitive) gut and hollered, "I don't like it when people call me Bird Brain! That's not my name!"

The vine wound up a few more feet.

As the vines lifted Gabe, the EarthWorm Pachyderm snapped into action again, realizing its competitor was getting away. The blobby beast started squirming forward, and there was much honking and grunting and gnashing of teeth. Gabe was only about four feet away from the top now, but the EarthWorm Pachyderm was so big that it could still reach him with its snout. One smack, and Gabe, who was barely hanging on, would tumble right onto its slimy back.

"Okay, okay, I'm sorry!" Rafi shouted. "I didn't mean it. I'm just really freaked out. Let's pull!"

At these words, the vine yanked itself upward again. Milton and Rafi pulled, and the vine continued to spin, like they were all somehow working together, boys and plant. They pulled and spun and pulled and spun.

Until finally Gabe came clambering out of the hole.

131

"Hey hey," he said, collapsing into a bloody, dusty, grinning heap. "Didja see that monster down there? Yikes!"

Rafi didn't waste any time. He scooped his brother up, jumped to his feet, and started toward the beach.

But then he paused and turned back around. "Thanks, Sea Hawk," he said before hurrying away.

"You are most welcome," Milton said to the boys' retreating figures. Then he slumped to the ground (a safe distance from the cave-in).

It was some time before he was able to roll over and crawl back to the hole. The EarthWorm Pachyderm wasn't there anymore. If this were *Isle of Wild*, this would be the time to observe this magnificent(ly grotesque) creature more fully and complete a field journal entry. So he watched and waited, even dropping in a few pieces of the meatball he'd packed in one of his zippered pockets for an afternoon snack. No elephant-worms were forthcoming, however, so finally, he headed back to the beach.

It was only when he reached Uncle Evan's front porch that he realized Rafi still had the field guide.

CHAPTER 31

Solutions in the Dark

That night, Milton couldn't sleep.

His insides were a mishmash, a smorgasbord of feelings, a hodge-podge of thoughts both rotten and spectacular—which made sense because it had been a mishmash-smorgasbord-hodgepodge kind of day.

On the one hand, he had run toward a cry for help with only the slightest bit of hesitation. On the other hand, Fig had basically said she didn't want to be his friend anymore.

On the one hand, he had proved himself Sea Hawkian, rescuing a small child in peril and insisting upon correct (fake) name usage. On the other hand, Rafi had stolen the field guide.

On the one hand, he'd spotted a never-before-seen creature. On the other hand, the creature had vanished just like the Sweet Pickle Tree, so what did it even matter?

Also, there were basically monsters living under the ground. Maybe under this very cottage.

He was half-awake, contemplating the spectaculous on one hand and the rotten on the other, when a noise startled him into full awakeness. He sat up on the pull-out couch-bed, shoved his glasses on, and glanced around the room. There was nothing there.

Then he heard something tapping on the front door. Something, perhaps, like an enormous, slimy trunk.

"The EarthWorm Pachyderm has come for me," Milton whispered into the darkness.

"It's Fig!" came a voice through the crack in the door.

Milton let out a sigh of relief (it had been a tense seven seconds) and went to open the door.

Outside, the air was gusty and sprinkled with random Incredible Symphonic Cicada notes. The full moon lit up a path through the ocean and right to Fig, who was grinning and clutching her notebook.

"What are you doing here?" Milton asked, stepping onto the porch. And then, "I'm sorry I yelled at you. I should have helped with the misspelled words!"

Fig shook her head. "You shouldn't have," she said. "That was the point. I needed some time alone. It really is okay for us to do things apart."

"When you say that," Milton said, "do you secretly mean you never want to do anything with me ever again?"

"Seriously, Sea Hawk? I'm here at your front door," Fig replied, "seeing you right this second. I'm here in the middle of the night because I couldn't wait until morning to talk to you. What do you think?"

Milton only had time to consider these (very illuminative) facts for a few seconds before Fig said, "Anyway, I figured it OUT!"

This last part was a joyful and entirely too loud screech.

"Shhhh!" Milton shushed her. "Do you want to wake up the whole island?"

"I was right!" Fig whisper-yelled, shoving her notebook at him. "The misspelled words are clues! The missing letters—they form a message!"

Milton took the notebook from her. She grinned over his shoulder while he read:

```
1.  adridged—aBridged  B
2.  arr—arE  E
3.  tis—tHis  H
4.  magnifycent—magnifIcent  I
5.  comserved—coNserved  N
6.  janger—Danger  D
7.  put—But  B
8.  feer—feAr  A
9.  jumgle—juNgle  N
10. vou—You  Y
```

135

11. treesure—treAsure A

12. islard—islaNd N

13. prodected—proTected T

14. fwee—fRee R

15. yoo—yoU U

16. dhe—The T

17. wittin—witHin H

18. pagez—pageS S

19. yuu—yOu O

20. broved—Proved P

21. earnud—earnEd E

22. simcerely—siNcerely N

BEHIND BANYAN TRUTHS OPEN

"Egad. You really did it," Milton said. "You cracked the code!"

Fig opened her mouth in a silent scream of happiness. She jumped up and down, and Milton joined her.

After a few moments of calisthenic joy, they settled onto the lawn chairs with the notebook between them.

"*Behind Banyan Truths Open*," Milton read out loud again. "What's that supposed to mean? And there are lots of banyans on this island. I wonder which one Dr. Paradis is talking about?"

"It's got to be the tree ship one," Fig replied. "It's the biggest by far."

"We haven't looked at the vines there yet," Milton said. "You know, for . . . reasons. But I actually encountered that reason today, and it's quite the tale, if I do say so myself."

He told Fig about the EarthWorm Pachyderm and how he and Rafi had rescued Gabe from the hole with the vine's help and how Rafi had actually said both *I'm sorry* and *Thank you.* The only part he left out was the stolen field guide. He didn't want to put a damper on the night's amazingness.

"I don't know which part is more unbelievable," Fig said when he was finished. "Although I doubt it means Rafi will be happy to see us by the tree ship. But that's just too bad for him." She smiled, a flash of bright in the moonlight. "Okay, I'm going to go back home and get some sleep. We have a lot to figure out tomorrow."

She hopped up and headed for the beach road. And as Milton watched his friend walk toward her sunshine door, with a sky full of stars and the soft soundtrack of an insect symphony, he felt happier than he had in a long, long time.

"So long, Fig!" he cried, completely forgetting to whisper. "Until we meet again."

"So long, Sea Hawk!" Fig called, turning to wave at him. "See you in the morning!"

CHAPTER 32

Missing!

Milton's alarm went off at 6:15 the next morning. He rose from his couch-bed, suited up, and was about to head out the door when he realized—

There were no noise coming from Uncle Evan's room.

Other than Milton's first day and the day of the hike, Uncle Evan had been fast asleep (and earsplittingly loud) when Milton arose every morning. Milton peeked behind the beaded curtain, wondering if his uncle had found some miracle cure for his nightly respiratory racket.

But the bed was empty. Uncle Evan was gone.

Milton checked the icebox, but there was no note. Feeling a bit disconcerted at his summer guardian's disappearance, he headed to the Morris cottage, where Fig was slipping out her front door.

"Hey, Sea Hawk," she said. "Ready to go to the banyan?"

"Oh . . . yes," Milton said distractedly. "Ready."

They continued together up the beach path, passing the Alvarez cottage. Gabe was alone outside. He had bandages on his knees and elbows and one on his forehead, but as he was currently doing somersaults through the little front garden, he appeared to be in good health overall.

"Hey hey, Sea Hawk!" he cried. "Hey hey, Fig! Are you looking for Dr. Greene? He went that way!" Gabe pointed toward the barely there trail that led to Dr. Paradis's house. "Are you going there? Is something happening? I'll come too! Let me get Rafi."

"Ah. You don't have to—no need!" Milton called after him.

"What's going on, Sea Hawk?" Fig asked. "Dr. Greene's at Dr. Paradis's old house?"

"I suppose," Milton replied. "He was already gone when I woke up this morning, which is most unusual. He didn't leave a note either."

Instead of going up, Fig's eyebrows pulled down, her eyes compressing with worry. "We should check on him," she said.

They took the barely there trail through the unshaded, super bright meadow of dune grass (thank heaven for explorer hats) and then through the (blessed) shade of the towering trees that surrounded the dilapidated home of the deceased Dr. Paradis. Milton would have gone to the back of the house, where Uncle Evan had told him he went when he needed to think, but Fig climbed the stairs to the sagging porch.

The paint-chipped front door, Milton now saw, was ajar.

Without hesitation, Fig pushed the door open, and Milton followed her over the threshold. The inside of Dr. Paradis's old house was as crumbly and neglected as the outside. The floorboards were probably varnish-shiny once, but now they were cracked and dull. The wallpaper was peeling and discolored, and the whole place smelled musty and dusty and a tad rotten.

Milton and Fig tiptoed (it felt like a tiptoey kind of place) down the hall until it opened onto a small sitting room. The walls there were covered in sun-muted tapestries, and every square inch of floor space was filled with furniture—bamboo tables, a high-backed velvet settee, teak stools, a grand piano.

And sitting in front of a dust-coated rolltop desk, his shoulders hunched, his head hung low, was Uncle Evan.

Milton was reminded suddenly of the way his father had been slumped at the kitchen table one Saturday morning not long before he'd moved out. At the time, Milton had backed out of the kitchen, returned to his room, and crawled under his covers, playing *Isle of Wild* and completely forgoing meals until dinnertime.

Now he rushed forward. "Uncle Evan!" he cried. "What's wrong?"

Uncle Evan jumped to his feet. For a moment, it seemed like he might bolt for the front door. Maybe he would yell *So long* as he went. But then he sighed deeply and ran his hand over his face. "The court contacted me yesterday," he said. "They'll be making their decision on Friday. So I have until then to submit any final evidence supporting my petition for the island to be designated a protected wildlife refuge." He paused before continuing in a heavy voice: "Or I can submit papers formally withdrawing that petition."

Milton felt his sensitive stomach do a Gabe-style somersault. He was (somewhat uncharacteristically) speechless.

"Show him the field guide, Sea Hawk," Fig said, breaking the silence.

The field guide! Milton didn't think this was the most opportune time to tell Fig that the guide was no longer in his possession. He slapped at his empty zippered pockets. "Oh, I—I must have left it in the cottage! How silly of me," he said.

Fig frowned at him, then opened a pouch on her utility belt. "An Incredible Symphonic Cicada," she said, thrusting the jar toward Uncle Evan. "We found it by the river. That green thing in there with it is a fruit from a Sweet Pickle Tree."

"I saw the EarthWorm Pachyderm too," Milton added. "The elephant-worm-thing that lives underground. It's real, Uncle Evan. Rafi and Gabe saw it too. We can write about it and send our report to the courts as proof!"

He'd been sure his uncle would cry from happiness when he finally learned that the never-before-seen creatures were real. But now . . . well, Uncle Evan *did* look like he was going to cry, but Milton was 100 percent sure that happiness didn't have anything to do with it.

It wasn't exactly the triumphant reveal he'd hoped for.

"There's nothing I can do," Uncle Evan said, staring down at the pickle-juice-sucking, tiny tuxedo-wearing bug in his hands. "We haven't been able to get a specimen in a long time, so I'm sure the Alvarezes will be thrilled, but the cicada is—it isn't new. And the other creatures—I've worked nonstop for years studying the vine and the island. I've brought the best environmental minds here. I've spent these last few months scouring our notes and research, but nothing I've come up with has been enough." He handed the bug jar back to Fig and shrugged both shoulders. "Dr. Paradis told me the island was waiting, but it obviously wasn't waiting for me. I think it's time to give up."

If Milton had thought Uncle Evan looked smaller on the docks ten days ago, it was nothing compared with the way he looked now. It made Milton's heart ache and his stomach clench. If only he could give his uncle some Sea Hawkian vim and vigor. "Uncle Evan," he started, "you don't mean—"

"Can Sea Hawk and I go camping?" Fig interrupted.

Uncle Evan lifted his head slightly. "Camping?"

"Like . . . sleeping outside?" Milton asked Fig.

"Yes," she said. "Camping. Tonight. I want to do some overnight observations for the nature survey. We can stay in the tree ship."

142

Uncle Evan shrugged again. "I guess," he said. "It's fine with me. You'll have to ask your mom, of course."

"I will. I'll go ask her now," Fig agreed, but she didn't turn to go. Instead, she leaned forward and gently set the bug jar on the rolltop desk. "You should know," she said, "that my mother told me how hard you've been working to save the island. And for what it's worth, she isn't sorry we came here. This island was exactly what she needed."

Milton thought he saw Uncle Evan give Fig his smallest smile at these words, but it faded so quickly that he couldn't be sure.

CHAPTER 33

Pack It Up, Ship It Out

"So why are we going camping?" Milton asked Fig as they headed back down Dr. Paradis's hall.

"Because we're getting that treasure," Fig said, her words timed to her fast-paced footsteps, "no matter what. Today is Wednesday, so we have today and tomorrow to figure out how to get behind that tree ship banyan."

"We're still going to save the island!" Milton cried. He took off his hat and threw it into the air as they stepped onto the sunshiny front porch.

Where Rafi and Gabe were waiting for them.

"Why do you have that?" Fig demanded, pointing to the field guide in Rafi's hand. "Sea Hawk, how did Rafi get the guide?"

"I took it yesterday," Rafi said. He held the leaf-paged book out to Fig, who snatched it up. "Me and Gabe read the whole thing last night, and I don't know if any of it's actually real, but we want to help."

"Treasure, me mateys!" sang out the patched-up Gabe.

Milton glanced from Fig to Rafi, from Rafi to Fig, and even though his sensitive stomach was beginning to curl into itself, he didn't feel like fleeing the scene quite yet. Maybe it was because he had assisted in a life-and-death rescue mission. Maybe it was because he had (very impressively) stood up for himself. Maybe it was because Rafi had (somewhat shockingly) actually apologized. Maybe it was all of these things, but something, Milton felt, had shifted between them.

Fig, however, had not been part of Operation Rescue Gabe.

"Just because Sea Hawk was careless with the guide and also lied to me"—she paused to frown at Milton, who gave her his most sincerely penitent look—"doesn't mean we need help."

Rafi let out a *pshaw* of duck-lipped frustration. "We heard what you and Dr. Greene were saying," he said. "You only have two days to find Dr. Paradis's treasure. You definitely need help."

Fig ignored him. "Come on, Sea Hawk," she said. "*We* have an island to save."

Rafi threw up his arms and stomped off the porch. "Come on, Gabe!" he called. "We'll see who gets the treasure first!"

A few minutes later, Milton burst through the front door of Uncle Evan's cottage. His instructions from Fig were to pack for a night outdoors and then meet at the tree ship in twenty minutes. He got to work filling his canvas backpack with supplies.

He would be wearing his utility belt (obviously), which covered a lot of camping basics. There was also some useful gear on the makeshift shelves that lined Uncle Evan's walls, and Milton decided that given the circumstances, Uncle Evan wouldn't mind if he helped himself. He took a sleeping bag that was stuffed in an impossibly small pouch and a waterproof sack that he thought would come in handy in case of inclement weather. He considered bringing a few cans of spaghetti and meatballs, but they were super heavy. He did find some packages of what looked like grayish beef jerky and a packet of crumbs that had probably been crackers once. He hoped Fig was packing extra snacks.

He still had lots of room in his backpack, but he wasn't sure what else to bring. He had only camped that one time with Uncle Evan, and, being five years old then, his mother had done his packing for him. Finally, he added an extra pair of socks and a fork, and, after some serious back-and-forth, he tucked his HandHeld into the dry bag too. Just in case.

That oughta do it.

Because his packing had only taken five minutes, he did a few stretches (maybe being limber and loose would help him keep up with Fig) before he shouldered his pack and headed out the door with eleven minutes to spare.

146

The sun was shining, the waves were crashing, a pelican was swooping over the water, and Milton felt like the world was his oyster (whatever that meant).

"The adventure is now!" he shouted as he took off down the beach trail toward the banyan tree and the treasure that surely lay beyond.

CHAPTER 34

Truths Open, Indeed!

Fig arrived at the tree ship a few minutes after Milton, and she had a lot more supplies than he did. Milton thought he'd probably collapse in T-minus ten seconds if he had all that gear on his back.

In spite of her obvious preparedness, Fig looked nervous. She was flipping the field-guide pages back and forth and poking at the vines. Milton wasn't sure he'd ever seen Fig nervous. It put a bit of a damper on his oyster-world feeling.

"Now that we're here, I don't know what to do," Fig admitted. "I mean, we know the vines can move, but what kind of a clue is *Truths open*? What truths? I feel like we're still missing something."

To be honest, Milton had expected that Fig would have figured that out by now. Fig was always figuring things out.

But as he stood next to her studying the green wall, Milton realized that actually he was the one with the most vine experience.

He had seen the vines move three times now—when he found the field-guide box, by the Sweet Pickle Tree, and when he and **Rafi** saved Gabe. The question was *why* had the vines moved? The only thing he could think of was that on all three occasions, he had been talking when the vines rolled up.

"The vine is *always willing to listen*," he said to himself, remembering the field-guide entry.

It wasn't much to go on, but he would give it a shot. What should he say though? What would Sea Hawk say to make these vines part?

Milton took a deep breath, puffed out his vest-covered chest, and cried, "Come now, my good vines. Show us the treasure beyond!"

If he really were Sea Hawk, there was no doubt those vines would have parted before his brawny, dashing incredibleness.

But they didn't.

Milton glanced at Fig, then moved closer to the vines, until he could only see green and white. "Hello, vines," he whispered. "Can you let us through, pretty please?"

The vines didn't move.

Milton reached out to touch the tiny white flowers and the friendly leaves. "Do you remember me?" he continued. "I'm the one who told you that I used to ruin things and that I didn't want to be called names anymore."

As if in response, the vine rose up off the ground. It was only a few inches, like an old-timey lady lifting her skirts to walk through a puddle. But those few inches were Milton's answer.

"Fig!" he cried, spinning around, super intense-faced. "Tell me something true!"

"Um, okay," Fig said. "Dr. Paradis first set foot on the Lone Island after her sailboat was blown off course on the way to Ascension Island."

Milton swung back to the vines.

They were motionless.

"Not that," Milton said, turning to Fig again. He pressed both hands to his explorer hat as he reviewed each vine-roll-up incident. Yes, the things he'd said to the vines had been truths, he realized, but not facts. "It has to be something true about you!"

"My favorite color is marigold?" Fig offered.

Milton didn't even have to check to know the vines were not going to be impressed. "Fig," he cried, "it has to be a truth about you that you wouldn't tell just anyone. Something you care about. The vine is *always willing to listen to those who have nothing to hide.*" The vines shivered in that unfelt breeze (which Milton now suspected was not a breeze at all) and brushed against his hand. "And you have to be touching them!" he added, remembering how the vines had ripped out of his grasp each time. "It's like—it's like a botanical lie detector test. So grab ahold and spill your guts to the foliage, Fig!"

"Seriously, Sea Hawk?" Fig said, but she approached the vines.

The flowers blossomed ever so slightly as she lifted a strand and wound it around her hand. Then she let out a cry of surprise as the tendril began to move on its own, twining gently around her wrist, like it was taking her pulse. "Okay," she said a little warily. "Here goes. I—I'm happy on this island, and my mother is too. I don't want to leave."

As soon as Fig stopped speaking, the wall of vines began to quiver like it had when Milton found the field guide. The vines shook. They shivered. Then they began to part.

A path opened up in the wall of green.

"*Behind banyan truths open*, indeed!" Milton shouted, pumping a fist in the air.

Suddenly, the vines began to twitch and a few dropped back into place. The vine door was closing.

"Hurry!" Fig cried.

She rushed through the opening, with Milton right behind. They ran for about ten feet, but then they met another Truth-Will-Out Vine wall. Behind them, a layer of vines had swung shut. They were trapped!

"It's your turn, Sea Hawk," Fig said. "Quick—tell a truth!"

"Me? Ah, yes. Of course. No problem," Milton replied.

It was a problem though. It was a big problem.

He could, of course, tell Fig that he was not who he had been claiming to be this whole time. He could confess his lies . . . but he really didn't want to, because he didn't want to stop being Sea Hawk. Not yet.

So what truth would Sea Hawk tell? Probably a not-too-big-of-a-deal, humble-brag kind of truth (*Sometimes I think I may be too strong!* or *I have occasionally gotten hand cramps while completing my exceedingly brilliant field journal entries!*). Or maybe, being the epitome of awesome, he didn't have any truths to tell.

Milton decided to go with that. He grabbed a handful of vines, cleared his throat, and declared, "I am an open book, Vine. I have no truths to reveal."

The vines did not stir.

"Why don't you try again?" Fig said. "I'm sure you can think of one little truth."

The truths that came to Milton were not little though. They were very big and very rotten and very definitely not humble-brags. They were things he didn't want to even think about, let alone say out loud. But he had tried the Sea Hawkian approach twice now with no success, and Fig was waiting.

So Milton adjusted his explorer hat about six times, held tight to a green strand, and finally blurted out, "It may shock you to know this, Vine, but currently Fig is my only friend in the entire world."

The vines split again.

Milton and Fig ran farther this time, so that when they came to another vine wall they were more than thirty feet in. Milton wondered exactly how long this would last. He had a vest-covered heart-stopping moment where he imagined Fig and himself trapped in the Truth-Will-Out Vine for days, telling secret after secret until they died of thirst . . . or embarrassment.

Fig's voice snapped him out of it.

"Before Sea Hawk got here," she said, "I hadn't had any friends in a long time. And I didn't really want any."

The last of the vines parted.

CHAPTER 35

It's a Jungle in Here

There was a historic theater that Milton and his mother used to go to. Not in the last year or so, not since things had started getting so tense and sharp. But before that, the theater had been the place they went for special days, sitting side by side with a bucket of popcorn between them and nothing else. The theater showed old movies—black-and-white films, silent films, musicals, that kind of thing. At the front, there was a red velvet curtain, and before the movie started, symphony music (probably made by instruments, not bugs) would pipe through the speakers. As the final notes ended, the curtains would pull back, revealing the great screen behind it, already lit up with the first flickering scenes of the film.

It was like that now as the vines split. Like a show had just started.

The Lone Island Show, starring Sea Hawk and Fig.

"Great flapping falcons!" Milton cried. "We did it!"

The jungle behind the vines was an incredible sight. It was full of plants that Milton recognized but had never seen in the real world before. There were rubber trees and magnolias, cacao trees and Spanish bayonet, and palms of every variety. There were bromeliads and orchids springing from tree trunks, along with the occasional clump of Truth-Will-Out Vine. The ground was thick with brush and wildflowers and creeping vines.

"The field guide was right," Milton said, stopping to observe an enormous, vividly violet flower. "The vines weren't destroying the island. They were protecting it."

"So many people over the years have wanted to turn this island into something else," Fig said. "I guess detecting the truth is the vine's survival adaptation."

"Like a test you have to pass to prove you don't have *questionable intentions*," Milton said, remembering Dr. Paradis's words.

The air was heavier on this side of the Truth-Will-Out Vine, humid and hot. There were so many trees and they were so close together that not much sunlight could get through. It was as dark as late evening, even though it was only midmorning, which made the jungle seem mysterious and strange (and awesome, Milton thought).

Even as dark as it was, it was a lot lighter than it should have been.

"Look, the vines aren't above us either!" Fig said, her head thrown back.

155

Milton remembered something, something he had forgotten because of turbulence and the possibility of regurgitation. "When I was flying here," he said, "I thought I saw the island moving. Well, the vines, I mean. You couldn't see any of this, even from above."

"So the vines can cover the whole island," Fig said.

"And no one can even see what they're missing," Milton said, shaking his head in amazement. Then he surveyed the seemingly solid mass of foliage ahead of him. "We are truly in uncharted territory. Shall we go . . . onward?"

"Yes. I'm not exactly sure which way though," Fig replied, but her nervousness from earlier didn't return. "I didn't know what we'd find behind the banyan. Let's keep moving inland for now."

"An excellent plan," Milton said readily, wiping his already-sweaty forehead. "Lead the way, Fig."

As they hiked, Milton was in a state of constant elation. He couldn't be more Sea Hawkian than this, trekking through the jungle on the trail of never-before-seen species. However, if this were *Isle of Wild*, he would be running at top speed, vaulting over fallen logs, swinging on lianas.

There was no running, vaulting, or swinging here. Moving through the jungle was hard work. The wildflowers on the ground were pretty, but Fig and Milton kept tripping over their trailing stems. Milton got snagged on at least a dozen super sharp briar bushes, and it seemed like every possible route led to a dead end, so they spent a lot of time backtracking.

After about an hour of slogging along, Milton's elation had evaporated, and he was so sweaty that it looked like he had been swimming, not walking. He was glad he'd brought the extra pair of socks. At least one part of him would be dry when they stopped for the day.

To keep morale up (mostly Milton's since he was the one who kept trying to sit down for *just the tiniest rest*), Fig read aloud from the field guide during the less taxing parts of the trek. It kind of helped to take Milton's mind off how exhausted he was and how unfun this scientific expedition had very quickly become. But not really.

After another hour of trekking, they came to a river. Fig said it was *their* river, the one that flowed into the bay. Milton thought she probably knew what she was talking about, but it was hard to believe. The river that flowed into the bay was a thin, trickling thing. This part of the river was more than fifty feet across, murky, and very deep, by the look of it.

The good thing about the river was that there weren't a lot of plants growing on its banks, so the path was much clearer.

The bad thing about the river was that its banks were made of incredibly thick, sticky, stinky, sludgy mud that tried to suck them down with every step.

Six of one, half a dozen of the other, really.

"I can't walk any longer," Milton gasped after only fifteen minutes of mud-trudging. "My boots are full of muck. My lungs are collapsing. My legs are turning into jellyfish. We've got to take a break!"

"It's not time for another break, Sea Hawk," Fig called, squelching onward.

"But my legs!" Milton cried, completely forgetting that he was supposed to be made of brawn and steel and incredibleness. "My le-e-e-e-egs!"

Fig came to a sudden stop. "How do your arms feel?" she asked.

Milton held them out for inspection. "Well, they're not likely to win any Brawniest Appendages awards," he said. "But I guess they're okay. Why?"

Fig pointed down the river. Up on the bank, with only its faded red nose showing, there was a canoe.

CHAPTER 36

Rollin' on the River

The canoe had obviously been left there some time ago. Dr. Paradis had been dead for six years, and she'd been really, really old when she died, so it wasn't super likely she'd been going on any wild river-rafting adventures in her final years. The canoe was aluminum, and it was partially buried under some fallen palm fronds and river detritus, but it wasn't too hard to dig out. There was even a silver paddle underneath.

"Dr. Paradis mentions canoeing in the guide, remember?" Fig said as she dragged the canoe down the riverbank. "I bet that was a clue! She must want us to follow the river."

Milton bobbed his head back and forth. "I guess," he said. "But she mentioned it in the *Push-Pull Centopus* entry. What if we run into that thing?"

"Let's see if the canoe floats," Fig said, "and worry about that later."

She climbed into the canoe while Milton held it still. After a few bounces, the vessel hadn't sunk or even leaked.

"We have buoyancy!" Milton cried, lifting his arms in victory.

Fig jumped into the shallow water. "I don't like that there aren't any life vests," she said as they pulled the canoe back to shore. "We'll have to be very careful. There's also only one paddle, and . . . I kind of think I should be the one to use it."

"Having never canoed before," Milton replied, "I am in full agreement."

After a quick lunch of granola bars and apricots (Fig had, in fact, packed extra food so Milton didn't have to start on the grisly gray jerky quite yet), they prepared to set sail (so to speak). Milton found a big branch that he thought would make a perfect second paddle. It had lots of little twigs that he was sure would move the water more efficiently. He checked to be sure the dry bag was secure, then clambered into the front of the canoe.

Then, with a push and a jump from Fig, they were off.

The tide must have been going out, because the current was against them as Fig paddled up the wide, deep river. In spite of his lingering fears about cephalopods potentially lurking in the murky shallows, Milton was in much better spirits now that they weren't walking anymore. He didn't even feel that seasick (riversick?).

"Are you going to paddle?" Fig asked from the back of the canoe.

"I don't think it'll make much of a difference," Milton replied. "I'm not known for my upper body strength."

"At least pretend," Fig said.

Milton shrugged. "If it will make you feel better." He trailed his branch over the side. The twigs dragged in the water. The canoe drifted off course.

"Okay, stop pretending," Fig said with a laugh.

For a while, there was silence and hard work (on Fig's part). Milton's thoughts wandered, but not to his same old rotten thoughts. Instead they wandered to the incredibleness he'd witnessed at the vines—and the truths he and Fig had told.

"I don't mean to pry, Fig," he said, "but I find it difficult to believe that someone of your caliber would ever be without friends."

Milton kept facing frontward, but he could hear Fig's paddling slow. "Well, I was. After my dad . . ." She trailed off, and when she spoke again, her voice was lower and sort of heavy. "After he died, I was really sad, and I guess not exactly fun to hang out with. All my friends were really awkward and weird around me. And then I found out they were having sleepovers and birthday parties without me. So I decided I didn't care. I didn't need friends."

Milton found that he could understand this decision. After the Bird Brain Incident, he had stopped trying to get Dev to be his friend again. He had stopped trying to get anyone to be his friend. But he

161

had still *wanted* friends. He had wanted them desperately. Maybe it would have been easier—would have hurt less—if he could have just said *I don't care.*

"When we moved here," Fig continued, "I started feeling better—happier. I was reading a lot though—*hiding in my books* is how my mother put it. She was always trying to get me to go outside. Then the Alvarezes showed up, and she was so excited for me to spend time with Rafi and Gabe."

"But you didn't want to?" Milton asked.

Fig sighed. She paddled once, but the canoe barely moved. "Things didn't start off well. I used to spend a lot of time in the tree ship—reading mostly—and then one morning, Rafi was there, and he didn't want to be on the island, and—" She sighed again, louder this time. Her paddle was motionless. "It wasn't a good combination, I guess."

"I'm sorry, Fig," Milton said.

"Like I said, it doesn't bother me," Fig replied. The canoe jolted forward as she gave a tremendous push. "I don't care."

Milton knew this wasn't true. He knew, in fact, that the opposite was true. But, again, he understood not wanting to care. There were plenty of things he wished he didn't care about.

And this, he realized, was the time to tell Fig about them. She had told her truths. Now he needed to tell his.

That was how it worked, wasn't it? When someone reached out

their hand to you (metaphorically speaking, since Fig was paddling right now and her hands were otherwise occupied), you were supposed to reach out your hand too. Both hands had to move or neither one would get held.

"I don't know exactly how you feel, of course," Milton said, "but I will tell you that I had the Most Totally, Terribly, Horribly, Heinously Rotten Year of All Time. I'm not sure that I want to discuss every horrendous detail, but perhaps you would like to hear some of it?"

"If you want to tell me, you can, Sea Hawk," Fig replied.

"I don't want to," Milton said. "I don't want to think about it at all. In fact, I've been trying my best *not* to think about it. But you're my best friend right now, Fig, and if you can't tell your best friend the truth about the rotten stuff that happens to you, who can you tell? So here is the story of the Bird Brain Incident."

CHAPTER 37

The Bird Brain Incident

The Bird Brain Incident had happened like this:

It was November. Milton had been in sixth grade for less than three months, and even though he had not officially christened the year the Most Totally, Terribly, Horribly, Heinously Rotten Year of All Time, it definitely already was. Dev had started spending occasional lunches with his new friends. Milton's parents' arguments had gotten more frequent and louder. Milton brought his HandHeld to school every day.

On the Bird Brain Incident afternoon, he was playing *Isle of Wild*, hiding his HandHeld under his desk in Science class. Sea Hawk was prowling through a particularly dense area of rain forest in search of a flower that could cure a deathly ill Dear Lady DeeDee. At the front of the room, Mr. Nelson was giving a lecture on taxonomy.

"There are 1.9 million named species on Earth," he said. "But scientists estimate there are more than 8.7 million unnamed species yet to be discov—Milton P. Greene. Whatever you're doing, stop. Focus."

Milton paused his game to make earnest eye contact with Mr. Nelson. "I'm totally focused," he assured his teacher.

Mr. Nelson continued with his lesson. "Each species is given a scientific or Latin name," he continued. "That name tells scientists where that organism fits into the—Milton, this is your last warning."

Milton paused his game again. "No more warnings required," he said. "Please continue discussing organisms and Latin names."

"Thank you," said Mr. Nelson. "Latin names. Right. Those names don't usually change, but they can. Scientists are always discovering new traits or new connections, and that information can lead to renaming."

Milton tried to pay attention. He really did. Science was his favorite class, and Mr. Nelson was his favorite teacher. But lately, it had become very difficult to concentrate, and after a few minutes, he pressed *Play* as discreetly as possible. Mr. Nelson's voice grew fainter and fainter, while the sounds of the rain forest filled his ears (despite the HandHeld being on *Mute*). Soon Milton was completely absorbed in hand-to-paw combat with a rabid Siberian tiger that had come leaping out of the underbrush while Sea Hawk was busy gathering tiny lavender flowers.

Then a hand reached out and grabbed the HandHeld.

Milton was so caught up in his game that in that instant, he was Sea Hawk and Mr. Nelson was the rabid Siberian tiger. He reacted (as he later explained to Ms. Wilks, the assistant principal), out of pure instinct.

And pure instinct told him to yank the HandHeld back with one hand while karate-chopping Mr. Nelson's nose with the other hand.

He had also let out the sharp, earsplitting, bird-of-prey call that Sea Hawk used to frighten off potential predators.

Having only taken that one karate class in his life, it was very unlucky that his chop was delivered so effectively. Blood gushed out of Mr. Nelson's nose immediately, and Milton really did not like blood.

So when the injured and thoroughly discombobulated Mr. Nelson made a second grab for the HandHeld, the nauseated and also thoroughly discombobulated Milton leaped to his feet and started running.

He ran and cawed across the room (with the soundtrack of his classmates' screams of horror and delight in the background), out the door, and all the way home, where he curled up under his covers and played *Isle of Wild* until his frantic parents arrived, took his HandHeld, and tried to force him to talk about what had happened.

The school had suspended him. He had to write an apology letter to Mr. Nelson (who had actually been very nice about the whole thing). He had lost his HandHeld for a month, although his parents were already too distracted to consistently enforce this. It was on his first day back after his suspension that those kids had surrounded him. The caws and shouts of "Bird Brain!" had been repeated with gusto several more times and then at random for weeks after. During that time, Milton had wished he could make himself invisible.

And then—it was like he was.

Dev seemed nervous even saying hello in the halls, like he was afraid the caw-ers would reappear any second. Kids Milton had been friendly with if not actual *friends* with avoided him. He escaped into *Isle of Wild* more than ever.

Yes, in a year of most totally terribly, horribly, heinously rotten things, the Bird Brain Incident stood out as one of the top two most totally terribly, horribly, heinously rottenest.

And now, for better or for worse, Fig knew all about it.

CHAPTER 38

Real-Life Adventure

"So there you have it," Milton finished. "That's why my vine truth was what it was—that you, Fig Morris, are my only friend in the whole entire world."

He had faced forward for his storytelling time (during which he had carefully avoided any mention of the name *Sea Hawk*) because he didn't want to see Fig's reactions. Now he could hear that her paddling had slowed again, but she remained silent. He sat quietly and watched the river flowing past and the clouds floating by. He sat and wondered if Fig was ever going to say anything or if perhaps he should dive into the river and let it carry him back to the beach.

"See, this is what I'm talking about," Fig finally said, breaking the stillness. "Something bad happens or you make one little mistake and you're done!" Milton peeked over his shoulder. Fig's eyebrows were down, and she was gripping the paddle tightly. "Dev sounds like some of my old friends."

"I behaved quite foolishly though," Milton said.

Fig shrugged. "So what? Everyone makes mistakes, don't they? Everyone gets nervous or sad or angry sometimes. Isn't that when you need friends the most? What's the point of friends who only stick with you when you're happy and doing everything right?"

"I suppose," Milton said. The sun felt warm on his face, and the breeze was gentle. "Although I think maybe—well, it's possible that I was a bit too distracted."

The canoe had started actually drifting backward, so Fig began her paddling again. "By the video game, you mean?"

"The very same," Milton agreed. "And by other things. Rotten things."

"Why do you think you played it so much?" Fig asked.

For Milton, the answer was obvious: *Isle of Wild* was awesome. There were dozens of new parts of the island to unlock, creatures to discover, missions to complete. And Sea Hawk was the coolest person in the virtual world. He was brave, handsome, and brilliant. He loved flora and fauna, knowledge and adventure, the jungle and his feline companion. What more could you want?

But hidden just behind all of that, there was more, like the jungle behind the vines. There was this: Milton's one-and-only friendship had started to crumble. He had been involved in a karate-chopping incident that had brought him school-wide notoriety. And for months, maybe for years, his family had been like a battered ship in a storm, a ship no one had been able to bail out or sail to safety until finally it had broken into pieces and sunk to the bottom of the sea.

That year, it had become very hard to be Milton P. Greene.

"Sometimes I want to be somewhere else, somewhere better," Milton told Fig, swiveling to see her. "And sometimes I want to be *someone* else too. Someone better."

Fig tipped her head to one side. "I like to be somewhere else and someone else too—that's part of why I like reading. But it can't be *better* if it's not real, can it?"

"It's real as long as I'm playing," Milton replied.

"But what about when you stop?" Fig asked. "What about when I close the book?"

"Therein lies the problem, I suppose," Milton said, turning back around.

He noticed now that the trees on the riverbanks had grown taller, and there were quite a few that he didn't recognize. The air smelled different here too, sharper, wilder. Fig paddled a few times, propelling them farther up the river, before she said, "Well, I'm glad we decided to come on this real-life adventure. Together."

Milton didn't trust himself to look at Fig. He wasn't sure what he'd do. He felt very strange inside, not bad but not great, sort of mushy and tender and vaguely nauseated.

"Indeed," he said. "Indeed, Fig."

"Because there are some real-life skills that you are seriously lacking," Fig continued, a smile in her voice. "Like how to paddle a canoe."

"*Isle of Wild* is an extremely educational game," Milton replied. "But you may be right that some of my experiential skills could use work. Let me remedy that." He stuck his branch in the river and gave a full-power push.

The canoe veered toward the bank. Laughing, Fig reached forward, grabbed Milton's branch, and threw it into the middle of the river.

"I changed my mind! No more paddling," she said with a grin. Then her smile faded. "What's that up ahead?"

Milton peered upriver. "Are those rapids?"

Fig was half standing in the back of the canoe now, craning her neck to see around him. Suddenly, she threw herself back down and gripped her paddle. "They're not rapids!" she yelled. "They're waves, and they're coming toward us. Get ready, Sea Hawk!"

CHAPTER 39

Wreckin' on the River

The first wave hit the canoe with a metallic *slap*! The canoe bucked and then lurched sideways as another wave hit. Fig tried to straighten the vessel, but the waves kept coming, faster now, bigger now.

Seconds later, water was everywhere—falling from the sky, spraying them in the face, filling up the canoe.

Milton had no idea what was going on, but he started trying to bail water with his explorer hat (was there anything that stunning accessory couldn't do?). He had done two scoops when he spotted something emerging from the river depths. Wiping his sopping-wet T-shirt sleeve across his glasses, he squinted ahead.

A wriggling, jiggling purple tentacle was waving through the air in front of the canoe. The tentacle ended in a sucker that was spewing out a fountain of river water. As Milton watched, another tentacle came popping up. Then another and another and another and soon the river was frothing and bubbling with the movement of a whole lot of tentacles.

Like, a hundred tentacles.

"It's the Push-Pull Centopus!" Milton screamed.

"Oh, really?" Fig yelled. "I hadn't noticed!"

She was paddling as fast as she could, trying to direct the canoe toward the shore, but the waves were so powerful that the vessel was at their mercy. It was rocking and tipping, sloshingly full of river water.

Milton thought he might throw up (the riversickness had arrived, full force).

"What did the guide say to do?" Fig asked frantically. "It had to do with the bird—the singing one. Sea Hawk, help me remember!"

"We're going to drown!" replied Milton, who was now crouched on the floor of the waterlogged canoe with his explorer hat over his eyes (yet another use—a blindfold in life-or-death situations!). "That centopus is going to suck us up and spew us out."

In spite of his terror and his screaming and his lack of paddling, Milton actually *was* trying to come up with a plan. But all he could think of was what Sea Hawk shouted when his health bar reached critical levels.

"Shall Sea Hawk perish thus?" he cried.

It was then that the singing started.

CHAPTER 40

La La La LAAAA!

"La!" belted out the voice. "La la! La la la! La la la LAAAA!"

The singing was coming from behind them but getting closer. Through the spewing, spraying, fountainous jets of water, Milton could make out a bright yellow smudge with two blobs inside—one big, one small.

"Hey hey!" yelled the small blob.

Milton rubbed his soaked T-shirt against his glasses again, and the blobs became—

Rafi and Gabe paddling toward them (and certain doom) in a canoe of their own!

Milton could hardly believe his eyes. And then he could hardly believe his ears.

"*Row, row, row your boat,*" Rafi started to sing (if the word *sing* were to mean *an earsplitting, terrible cacophony of mismatched sounds*).

It was, Milton thought, an unusual choice for last words.

"Come on, someone!" Rafi yelled. "Sing with me. We have to be Tone-Deaf Warblers!"

Tone-Deaf Warblers! Milton remembered what the guide said now. The bird's song would lull the centopus into a deep sleep, thus ending the sucking-spewing spree. Since there were no warblers around, Rafi was being one, and he needed their help.

Fig and Gabe answered his invitation. *"Gently down the stream,"* they sang.

But Fig's and Gabe's voices were unquestionably tuneful. They could have been in a choir. They could have been soloists. And that infuriated the centopus. At least it seemed to; it spewed about five hundred gallons of river water straight at them in response.

"Not you two!" Rafi spluttered. "You two be quiet. Sea Hawk, sing!"

Milton knew he was not a good singer. He had found out in first grade during rehearsals for the school play when a whole stageful of children had cringed and the girl next to him had actually wept at his vocalizations. The music teacher had quickly brought him a woodblock and a mallet. "Let's find another way to put your talents to use," she had said. "No more singing for you, Milton P. Greene."

And, he recalled with a growing sense of boldness, Sea Hawk had once engaged in an arm-to-tentacle tussle with a huge-eyed, many-appendaged cephalopod. It had taken quite a few *Restart*s,

175

but Milton had finally figured out that water beast's weakness—repeated, piercingly sharp caws.

Facing near-certain death in a sinking canoe, Milton realized that the time had come to cast off his woodblock-playing past. The centopus didn't like the sweet sound of harmonizing children's voices. The centopus liked cringe-worthy, weep-inducing, tone-deaf noise.

It was time to give it all he had.

"*Merrily, merrily, merrily, merrily,*" Milton sang as he rose from the canoe floor.

It sounded really, really awful.

The centopus loved it. It began waving its tentacles in time with the song (if the word *song* were to mean *a painfully loud, unmelodious series of ear-bleedingly horrendous vocalizations*).

"*Life is but a dreeeeeeeam!*" sang Milton and Rafi.

Milton finished the performance with a series of bird-of-prey calls that he felt sure Sea Hawk would have approved of.

The centopus expelled a final fountain of water, deflating its bulbous body. Tentacles still swaying, it sank back down into the river. There was a little gurgling sound, and then the water was still again.

"We did it!" Rafi yelled.

"Yes, we did," Fig said, dripping and wide-eyed in the back of the canoe. "But what are you doing here?"

CHAPTER 41

Expedition Crashers

Fig didn't wait for Rafi to answer. She pivoted their still sloshingly full canoe and paddled toward the shore. Milton's insides were wriggling and jiggling centopus-style as he watched Rafi and Gabe paddling after them in their yellow equally sloshy canoe.

When they reached the riverbank, Fig hopped out and tugged the canoe from the water without even waiting for Milton to disembark. "All right," she said, spinning around to face Rafi, who was attempting to help Gabe out. "How did you get here?"

"We were in the tree ship!" Gabe cried, ignoring his brother's hand and leaping onto the shore. "We saw you go through those vines. Wowzers, this mud is soooo squishy!" He pulled his foot up with a squelch and then shoved it back down again.

"So you followed us," Fig said.

"We didn't follow you," Rafi protested. "We went to the river, down where we saw you two the other day. The vines, uh, let us through there."

"I told the vines that I've been keeping a snake in Rafi's laundry hamper," Gabe said cheerfully, smooshing his feet up and down. "Rafi said he misses our old house and his old friends."

"The river must be like a—a back door," Milton posited. Rafi, meanwhile, busied himself with the buckles of his life vest, not looking at anyone.

"Then they can turn around and go right *back* through," Fig said, her eyes narrowed and her arms crossed.

Rafi straightened up, a scowl now creeping across his face. "No way," he said. "We're not getting in that river again. You really hate me so much that you want me to be centopus food?"

Fig's posture relaxed slightly. "No," she said. "I don't hate you, and I don't want that. But ever since you got here, you've been saying you can't wait to leave the island. Why would you even want to save it?"

Rafi unzipped his backpack and pulled out a dry bag. "Just because I don't want to *live* on the island doesn't mean I want it to be sold to someone who isn't going to take care of it," he said. He took his funny square camera out and started fiddling with its knobs. "Especially now that I've seen what's behind the vines. Plus Gabe wanted to come—"

178

"I sure did!" cried Gabe, who was now mud-spattered from his toes to his stomach.

Rafi put his camera cord over his neck and faced Fig and Milton. "Gabe and I were going to save the island ourselves, but now we're all here. So maybe we should do it together?"

Milton glanced over at Fig to find that her usually very readable face was a jumble of eyebrow ups and downs—which was exactly how Milton (and his stomach) felt.

When she finally spoke, Fig's voice was stern. "Let's get a few things straight," she said. "Sea Hawk and I are the ones who found the field guide and solved the clues. We're in charge. So if you're coming with us, we need to have some ground rules."

"I'm not following Dr. Bird Brain's rules," Rafi protested.

"The first rule," Fig continued loudly, "is absolutely no name-calling. What else, Sea Hawk?"

Milton turned to Fig with what he hoped was a why-are-you-doing-this-to-me expression. Since Operation Rescue Gabe, he wasn't exactly afraid of Rafi anymore, and if Fig was willing to let him join their adventure, then he could accept that. But he didn't want to set ground rules! Rafi might listen to Fig, but he would never listen to Milton.

Fig either didn't understand his super intense face (if only his eyebrows were as eloquent as hers!) or chose to ignore it. And as she gazed at him expectantly, Milton realized something.

This wasn't going to be like the Bird Brain Incident.

Fig was the kind of friend who would stick with him. If he needed help, she wouldn't watch from a distance. She would stand up for him. She would stand right next to him. He didn't need to be afraid at all.

So he adjusted his glasses, smoothed his (soaked and bedraggled) peacock feather, and said, "I agree with the no-name-calling rule, and also Fig and I are in charge of the field guide."

"Sea Hawk and I are in charge *period*," Fig amended. "We decide where we go and when we go there. Do you agree to these terms?" She put her hands on her hips and waited. Milton put his hands on his hips and waited too.

"Aye, aye, captains, my captains!" Gabe sang out.

"You're acting like I didn't save your lives two minutes ago," Rafi grumbled.

"We're very grateful," Fig said, "but the terms still stand."

For a minute, Milton wondered if Rafi wouldn't be able to handle those terms. Maybe he was going to storm back to his canoe in spite of the danger. But then he threw up his hands in the biggest shrug of all time and said, "Okay. Whatever. You two are in charge. Now can we get moving before something else in this jungle tries to kill us?"

It was Milton who replied. Hoisting his backpack, he took a deep breath and said, "Yes, I think we're ready to continue now. Onward."

180

CHAPTER 42

The World Upriver

Three hours upriver, the jungle had become a whole different world. There were very few plants that Milton recognized now (and he was pretty sure Fig didn't either). There was a kapok tree here, a flame tree there, a tamarind yonder, but the run-of-the-mill foliage had become few and far between.

Instead, there were tree trunks that were deep blue or iridescent or feather-covered, like giant birds. There were hanging flowers that shimmered like glass and tinkled like wind chimes. There were ginormous butterflies in every hue, polka-dot lizards, and birds with ten-foot-long tail plumage swooping and spinning across their path. Below their feet were blossoms with complex petals like origami, and vines that slithered, and pink-blue-purple crystals, which Milton thought must be the rock candy mentioned in the field guide (he didn't try to eat it though, for sanitary reasons). Everything was bright and brilliant and, to be honest, bizarro.

"Wowzers!" Gabe kept crying. "Wouldja look at that?"

"Wild and wondrous," Milton said. "Just like Dr. Paradis told us."

"Don't you feel like her right now, hiking through this place for the first time?" Fig said. She had been smiling ear to ear since they started hiking again, in spite of their new companions. "Think what could be in here—thousands of new species. And we get to find them all."

"It is pretty amazing," agreed Rafi, who had been snapping pictures nonstop.

Unfortunately, the incredible new flora was no easier to trek through. There were just as many poky thorns (including some that looked like chomping teeth), just as much thick underbrush (including some that fluffed up when they approached, like an angry cat's tail), and just as many dead-end routes.

It didn't help that they didn't really know where they were going either.

After the canoe hint, the only possible next clue Fig and Milton could find was the *Habitat* line in the *Astari Night Avis* entry: *Soaring through jungle canopy or nesting in the Starlight Starbright Trees, which incidentally, are the perfect trees to spend the night under.* They had been keeping an eye out for any trees that fit that description, while ignoring Rafi's repeated questions about where they were going. When they finally told him the plan, he was not impressed.

"We're going to wander around aimlessly until we spot some sparkly trees?" he said. "What if we miss them? Have you seen all the trees in here?" He gestured around, and Milton had to admit he had a point.

"Do you have a better suggestion?" Fig asked.

"Give me the field guide, and I will," Rafi replied.

Fig raised an eyebrow and marched ahead.

Rafi *pshaw*ed noisily. "May I *please* hold the field guide?" he called after her.

Milton pulled the guide from his dry bag and handed it to him. "You may hold it," he said in his most authoritative voice, "for half an hour."

Then he hurried to catch up to Fig before Rafi could respond.

As they hiked on, Fig found more and more things to ooh and ahh over, and Milton didn't feel so bad himself. Out here, in the wild, his thoughts were quieter, and his stomach wasn't nearly so blerghy. That old Nature Phase feeling was back in full force, giving him the sense that he was part of all this aliveness that surrounded him.

"It's weird," Fig said quietly as they passed a small clearing of spiral-shaped, rainbow-hued flowers, "I keep thinking about how much my dad would have loved this place."

Milton hesitated before he replied, not wanting to venture into Things You Do Not Say territory. "But he was an artist, not a scientist, right?" he finally asked.

"He was," Fig said, "but he mostly painted nature stuff. We would all go on weekend hikes together. My mother would collect plant samples, and he would paint, and I would read." She smiled, a small smile. "I haven't thought about that in a long time."

Milton paused as a winged lizard swooped across the path. "My parents went on expeditions with me too," he said. "Not far away, but to local parks. Not lately though. Uncle Evan claims that my father was once very outdoorsy, but now he pretty much just goes to work and then to his—his apartment." He shrugged. "Maybe that's one of the reasons he's been so unhappy."

"Has he been unhappy?" Fig asked, moving aside a palm frond from their path. And then another. And then another.

"I believe so," Milton said, thinking of how his father had become quieter and quieter and quieter, like someone being erased a little at a time. "I don't think—I don't think he got the adventure he wanted. I don't think Uncle Evan did either."

Fig nodded thoughtfully. "Maybe their adventure isn't over yet though," she said. "You never know what's going to happen next. Who could have predicted that your terrible year would end up here?" She gestured to the jungle surrounding them, and Milton had to admit, it was a pretty convincing argument.

"Not me," he said.

"No way!" Rafi suddenly screamed from behind them. "This spider has twelve legs!"

Fig hurried to see the spider, which was skittering across the open page of the field guide that Rafi had been reading. Milton waited where he was, thoughts still focused on unpredictable outcomes (and very intentionally not on too-many-legged insects).

"My parents would go nuts if they saw this," Rafi told Fig, holding the arachnid-topped leaf-page up to his camera.

"Yep," Gabe agreed. "They're entomophiles."

"Sounds like they're not the only ones," Fig said. Milton glanced over quickly (very quickly) and saw that Rafi was actually smiling at the (repulsive) creature.

"I wouldn't go that far," Rafi replied. "But I think me and this spider might have figured out another clue."

CHAPTER 43

GO TO THE CENTER

Ahead of them, on a small rise, there was a tree with huge leaves that attached to branches on both sides and sagged in the middle. They looked like dozens and dozens of hammocks, and Milton, who was in serious need of just the tiniest rest, beelined that way, saying, "Let's discuss this while we recline! Sans arachnid, please!"

The leaf hammocks were surprisingly soft and comfy, and Milton felt instantly better as he sank into the lowest one. Fig plunked down next to him, and Rafi and Gabe took the hammock across.

"Okay, Rafi, what did you find?" Fig asked, leaning forward.

Rafi opened the field guide with a flourish and held it between the hammocks. "I noticed," he said in a voice that Milton couldn't help thinking was a little ship-captainy, "that there are several words written in capital letters." He pointed to the *Astari Night Avis* entry. "See, here it says *GO*. That's the only thing in all capitals." He turned to the *Menu-You Bush* page next. "And here it says *TO*."

In the *UnderCover Cat* entry, he showed them the all-caps *THE*. And then finally, in the *Enmity-Amity Tree* entry was the last part of the clue:

Habitat: Even nearer to the
CENTER OF THE ISLAND

"See?" Rafi said triumphantly. "*Go to the center of the island.* It's a clue. I told you I'd be able to help!"

"I can't believe I never noticed that," Fig said, flipping through the pages herself. "But you're right."

Milton hadn't noticed it either, and right then he wished more than anything that he had. Fig got out her compass and determined their course, and then they were off again, toward the center of the island.

Less than an hour later, however, Gabe was starting to fall behind, and his elbow bandages had little spots of red coming through (yet another thing for Milton to avert his eyes from). Milton didn't have any EarthWorm Pachyderm–related injuries, but he was having a hard time keeping up too (probably due to exhaustion from all that paddling).

"It's going to be dusk in an hour," Fig said after Milton and Gabe plopped down onto the ground only ten minutes after their last break, "and it seems like we're already pretty far inland. Maybe we should think about setting up camp."

"Agreed," Rafi said before Milton could reply. "And look—do you think those are the Starlight Starbright Trees over there? Don't the leaves look star-shaped?"

"Unbelievable," Milton muttered. "Egad."

Because they did. The leaves were five-pointed and shimmery gold, spaced out on branches of gleaming silver. When they hiked closer, they saw that the trees grew in a circular copse with a flat, open space in the center. It was, as Dr. Paradis had pointed out, an excellent place to make camp, and Milton really wished that he had been the one to find it.

In a major wilderness-preparedness fail, he hadn't thought to bring a tent. Rafi had told his parents he was taking Gabe camping for one night, but he hadn't brought a tent either, because the Drs. Alvarez believed in open-air camping only—the better to see the sky and feel the earth—but also the better to be eaten alive by the Lone Island's killer mosquitoes. Luckily, Fig had them covered (literally).

"You don't need assistance, do you?" Milton asked as he watched her pulling tent poles and olive-green nylon out of the little bag she produced from her backpack.

"I've got it, Sea Hawk," she replied.

Milton, whose talents did not lie in assemblage of any sort, was relieved.

Until Rafi came over and started assisting in the assemblage, putting poles together left and right. He didn't even need to ask Fig for instructions!

Gabe was suddenly there too, gleefully pounding tent pegs into the ground with a rock.

"Here, allow me!" Milton said too loudly. He rushed over and yanked on one of the curving tent poles (they were supposed to be straight up and down, right?) and—

The whole thing collapsed.

Fig sighed. Rafi scowled and *pshaw*ed very noisily. Gabe kept banging the pegs.

"Okay. Well. I'm just going to scope out the perimeter," Milton said, backing away from all of them. "So long!"

He didn't run, but he did walk double time as he headed toward the edge of the clearing. There was a stream trickling along there, and he threw in some star-leaves and sticks that shimmered like tinsel. He could hear Fig, Rafi, and Gabe setting up the campsite, being all handy and outdoorsy without him. So much for him being in charge of anything.

Here was another problem Sea Hawk had never faced. Sea Hawk never had to prove anything to anyone. He was a lone explorer, his stomach was probably made of steel, and he could definitely set up a tent. He could make a shelter out of coconut husks and conch shells!

Milton tossed more tinsel sticks, feeling a little queasy, a little rotten, and a lot alone.

Then something fluorescent caught his eye.

Hanging low in the bushes were dozens of fruits, mango-like and vividly pink and orange. Milton recognized them from the field guide—they were from the Menu-You Bush—although it wasn't an entry he had spent much time puzzling over. He did remember that the fruits were delicious, and it occurred to him that this could be his redemption. He hadn't found the clues or the campsite or set up the tent, but he could forage their dinner, and wasn't that just as impressive—maybe even more so?

"Have I got a treat for you all!" he hollered as he plucked the fruits and loaded them into his explorer hat (yet another use!). He was so busy looking below that he didn't look above.

Where an enormous scarlet leaf-trap hung like a waiting open mouth.

"Come on over, everyone," he called. "I have fruit from the Menu-You Bu—AHHH!"

Milton P. Greene was swallowed whole.

CHAPTER 44

The Mishmash Inside

Milton had never been inside a human-size leaf-trap before. He doubted anyone had, in fact, even Sea Hawk (although Dear Lady DeeDee had once gotten trapped in the very sticky nectar of a pitcher plant, and Sea Hawk had had to find a horde of tree shrews to drink every last drop in order to free her).

Milton had hidden in a few places that year though.

He had hidden in the school bathroom, which was gross but also kind of cozy and surprisingly almost always empty (did no one pee at school?).

He had hidden in his room under his covers, sometimes while his parents had argued and sometimes while his parents stayed silent, seemingly forgetting, in both cases, that Milton was there at all.

He had hidden in *Isle of Wild*.

But still, bathroom stalls and blankets and virtual realities were one thing. The gooey, stifling, ripe-smelling innards of a carnivorous flora were quite another.

"HELP!" Milton screamed. "HELP!"

He could hear the faint sound of running feet and then Rafi's muffled voice calling, "Where are you?" He sounded, Milton was pleased to note, appropriately concerned.

"I'm in here!" Milton yelled, his own voice extraordinarily loud in the cramped space.

"Sea Hawk, are you—are you in the plant?" came Fig's voice, much closer.

"Yes!" Milton cried. "And I would like to exit immediately. Bring some tree shrews!"

"Yikes!" he heard Gabe chirp. "Is Sea Hawk inside that ginormous plant-mouth? How'd he get in there? Sea Hawk, why'd you go in the plant-mouth?"

"It was entirely unintentional!" Milton shouted back. "I was trying to procure us some dinner, and I ended up becoming dinner. And now I want out!"

"Hold on," Fig said. "I'm looking it up in the guide." There was silence except for some muted rustling, and then Fig cried, "Okay, listen! *Like its diminutive cousin the Venus flytrap, the Menu-You Bush will begin digesting its prey after five movements. The trap cannot be pried open from the outside, so if you happen to be on*

192

the Menu-You's menu, act with speed and deliberation and apply pressure to the petiole."

Milton had held his breath and remained motionless so that he could hear every word and now he was glad he had. Digestion! He was going to be digested! And how many times had he already moved?

"Sea Hawk, did you hear what you have to do?" Fig's voice was very slow, loud, and calm. "The petiole is the place where the trap connects to the stem. If you press on it, the trap will open. But you can't make too many movements."

Milton wanted to take a deep breath, but the smell of overly ripe mango and decomposition made him feel like pressure was already being applied—to his *stomach*. Now that his eyes were adjusting to the darkness, he could make out the rows of interlocked teeth in front of him and the mushy husks of ginormous insects stuck to the sides of the trap.

"I don't want to be digested," he said, hysteria beginning to overtake him in spite of Fig's best, soothing-voiced efforts.

"Sea Hawk!" Rafi yelled. "Pull it together. Apply the pressure."

"Shall Sea Hawk perish thus?" Milton howled, while remaining perfectly still.

"Sea Hawk!" Gabe screeched. "Get out of that plant-mouth."

"Who am I kidding?" Milton cried. "I'm no Sea Hawk! What kind of Bird Brain gets chomped up by foliage? This is the most totally,

193

terribly, horribly, heinously rotten thing that's ever happened to me. Let me out!"

"Sea Hawk P. Greene." It was Fig again, and she sounded like she meant business. "Listen to me, you kook. We can't let you out. You have to do it yourself. You *can* do it yourself. But you have to do it now."

Milton's heart was in his throat, and his stomach was in there too. But he trusted Fig. If she thought he could save himself, well, then he could (probably . . . hopefully). Listening to her didn't fix everything, of course (being that he was still trapped inside a carnivorous flora), but he started to feel . . . not Sea Hawkian exactly, but not Bird Brainy either.

Somewhere in between, maybe.

He didn't adjust his glasses because that would be an unnecessary movement that might lead to his immediate digestion, and he still couldn't take a deep breath for blerghing reasons. Instead, he crouched down in the trap (one movement), found the little dip where the trap met the stem (two movements), and pressed with all his might (three movements).

The trap snapped open, and Milton and a whole lot of glunk and glop came spilling out.

CHAPTER 45

Worth Being Eaten For

Milton went directly to the river. Fig brought him a tiny bar of soap that she had packed (who would ever think to bring soap?), and since he had only brought an extra pair of socks (which earned him a "Sea Hawk. Seriously?" from Fig), Rafi lent him a spare outfit.

"These are my only extra clothes," Rafi said, putting them on a rock. "So please try not to get eaten again."

"I shall do my absolute best," Milton promised.

Even though the last half hour had been truly harrowing, Milton was in good spirits after washing in the river. On the one hand, he had foolishly wandered into the maw of a carnivorous plant. But on the other hand, he had escaped using his brains, brawn, and bravery—and the help of his expedition mates.

Back by the (now assembled) tent, Fig had Milton's explorer hat. It was still clean (small blessings) and full of the fruits Milton had gathered before being ingested. They all leaned against the Starlight Starbright Trees and peeled back the fluorescent skins of what Dr. Paradis promised would be a true delicacy.

"Mine smells like mango," Rafi said, sniffing his fruit skeptically.

"Mine does too," Fig agreed. "Maybe Dr. Paradis was wrong about this one."

Milton's fruit smelled like mango too, and he didn't want mango. He also didn't want spaghetti and meatballs. What he wanted was pizza. Fresh, hot, cheesy goodness. Boy, wouldn't that hit the spot after what had most definitely been the most mortal-peril-filled day of his existence. His mouth was watering just thinking about it.

He supposed mango would have to do though.

He took a bite of the Menu-You Bush fruit.

And it tasted like pizza! Well, like juicy, mushy, kind of stringy fruit pizza, but pizza nonetheless. Milton thought it was the best meal he'd had on the Lone Island yet.

"This was almost worth getting eaten for," Milton said, grinning around the clearing as his fellow adventurers began to dig in.

"I wouldn't go that far," Fig said. "But it's pretty good to have tacos after a day like today. Even if they aren't exactly the right texture."

"You should try the spaghetti and meatballs!" suggested a juice-faced Gabe.

"Never!" Milton cried.

"That's what I have too," Rafi said. "It's our favorite."

"I may have to confiscate the remainder of these hard-won fruits if you're going to make such abysmal culinary choices," Milton told the confused brothers while Fig laughed.

It wasn't long after that the Incredible Symphonic Cicadas began tuning up for their song. The little tuxedoed musicians were all over the clearing, and the song they played was a complicated number with lots of sharp notes and trills and dramatic pauses.

Milton, Fig, Rafi, and Gabe sat together in the star-clearing and listened. Milton wasn't sure what everyone was feeling, but as he tapped his toes, he felt like he was part of that music too. He felt like he was part of the Lone Island.

CHAPTER 46

Reaching Hands

After the Incredible Symphonic Cicadas' song, everyone dove into the tent. The humming-bird-size mosquitoes tried their hardest to follow, but the nylon tent sides kept them out.

Milton set up Uncle Evan's sleeping bag between Fig and Rafi, with Gabe squashed on Rafi's other side. He considered taking another peek at the field guide and maybe trying to find another clue to really wow everyone with, but then he wriggled into his sleeping bag instead. He had never been so exhausted.

Everyone else must have felt the same way, because for a while, it was silent in the tent. All year, silence had been Milton's enemy. But he found that tonight, even though those same old rotten thoughts were still there, even though he had spent the day talking about his horribly heinous year more than ever before—tonight, he didn't mind the silence.

Tonight, the silence reminded him that he was here, here in the jungle in a tent with the rainfly folded up so that there was only a layer of mesh separating him from the sky. Here with thousands of stars shining down between the star-leaves of the trees that surrounded them. Here beneath a moon that was almost full and bluish white in the black sky.

He was here, and there was nowhere else he'd rather be.

As Milton watched the sky, he saw movement high above, as faint as a shadow. Then the moving shadow crossed the moon. For just a moment, the silhouette of a wings-outstretched bird was framed against the lunar glow. The bird shape was covered in gleaming points of light.

"I think that was an Astari Night Avis," Fig whispered.

"Did anyone see a shooting star in its tail feathers?" Rafi asked.

Milton had seen something, but he wasn't sure what. It could have been a shooting star. It could also have been the light from the real stars shining across the avis. But after the year he'd had, Milton thought he deserved a little luck, so he said, "I did."

"Did you make a wish?" Fig asked.

"Yes, indeed."

"Whadja wish for?" demanded Gabe, who appeared to be doing a headstand in his corner of the tent.

Milton thought he was going to reply *If you tell a wish, it won't come true.* But what actually came out of his mouth was . . . the truth. "I wished that my parents would stay together," he admitted. "They're getting a divorce."

Fig turned onto her side in her sleeping bag so that she was facing him. "I didn't know that," she said.

"I haven't made it common knowledge," Milton replied, still staring up. "But that's why they sent me here. They didn't think I could handle being around them. Or they couldn't handle being around me maybe. Probably both." He let out a sigh that came from the deepest depths of his sensitive stomach. "If ever there was a year that needed a *Restart*, it was this one."

Fig had opened her mouth to reply, when, much to Milton's surprise, Rafi spoke up. "I wouldn't mind a *Restart* either," he said. He didn't roll toward Milton and Fig, but he turned his face their way. "I used to actually like moving around all the time, but we stayed at our last site for three years, and I . . . I didn't want to leave. I wish I could go back."

"Then you wouldn't be with me!" Gabe hollered indignantly.

"Not by myself, Gabe," Rafi said. "You would come too, obviously. Anyway, we're supposed to go somewhere new in the fall, and my parents promised we would stay there for good, but they change their minds sometimes."

"They really love the—the bugs?" Milton asked.

"Yeah, but also this whole island," Rafi replied. "Because they're

200

scientists, but also because they think the island has, I don't know, like, special energy."

Rafi sounded embarrassed saying this, but Fig rose up to her elbows and peered over at him. "Maybe it does," she said. "We came here after my dad died, and my mother is . . . well, she's much happier than she was. And I am too."

"I didn't know your dad was dead," Rafi said. "I just thought he was . . . not here."

"It was a car accident," Fig replied. "Two years before we came to the island."

"I'm sorry," Rafi said quietly.

"I'm sorry too, Fig," Milton said.

"It was a long time ago," Fig replied. "It doesn't bother—" She cut herself off. Slowly, she lay back down, now facing the sky again. "It still bothers me sometimes," she said. "But not as much as it used to. And I'm sorry too. About your parents, I mean, Sea Hawk."

"Me too," Rafi said.

"And I'm sorry you had to leave your home, Rafi," Fig continued. "The Lone Island feels like home to me now, and I know I don't want to leave."

Milton wasn't sure what was happening right now. There was no Truth-Will-Out Vine in sight, but everyone was telling truths and reaching out hands, left and right.

"I think the worst part of the year, for me," he said to the sky and to his tentmates, "was how lonely the rotten parts were."

"You don't know lonely till you've lived on an almost-deserted island," Rafi said.

"Or thought about having to leave one," Fig added.

"You don't know lonely till you've given your favorite teacher a bloody nose in a terrible but unavoidable accident, lost all your friends, and then had your father move to a downtown apartment." Milton took off his glasses and rubbed his eyes, and when he opened them, the whole sky was a wild blur of colliding light and darkness. "But today I was sucked up and spewed out, I hiked farther than I ever thought possible, I was almost absorbed by a vicious flora, and it was both rotten and spectaculous. But not one bit lonely."

"That's because you're not alone," Fig said.

"Yeah," agreed Rafi, "like it or not, we're in this together."

"Together, my hearties," Gabe mumble-sang, a half-asleep lump now. "Whadaya think about that?"

"I think that may be the most spectaculous part of all," said Milton.

CHAPTER 47

In the Jungle, the Mighty Jungle

Milton lay awake long after everyone else had fallen asleep. All that heart-to-heart (to-heart-to-heart) talk had gotten him thinking about a whole new problem. He stared up at the stars (the ones that were leaves and the ones that were burning balls of plasma light-years away) and tried not to think anymore. He listened to the inhales and exhales of his three tentmates (and Rafi's snores, which were nothing compared with Uncle Evan's nightly hyena-laugh-walrus-grunt-kangaroo-coughs). He tried really hard to ignore the rotten thought that kept playing over and over and over in the stillness of the tent.

Finally, he couldn't take it anymore. He turned toward Fig and whispered, "Fig? Are you awake?"

Fig didn't answer, and when Milton scooted closer to her, he saw that her eyes were shut. She was breathing deep, fast-asleep breaths. But he needed to talk now.

So he positioned himself near Fig's ear and let out a bird-of-prey call. Not full volume, of course. Not very loud at all. Just loud enough. Then he rolled back over (lightning reflexes!).

Fig's eyes flew open. "What's going on?" she cried.

"Oh, hello, Fig," Milton whispered.

Fig gave a sleepy groan. "Why are you awake, Sea Hawk?" she muttered.

"I don't require much sleep," Milton replied. "Or maybe I do. But I have, at times, been able to survive on very little." He shifted in his sleeping bag so that he was facing her again. Without his glasses, she looked like an Impressionist painting, like a smudge in a world of smudges.

"Well, what is it?" she asked.

"I've been thinking, Fig," he said. "And the thing is . . . what if we *don't* find the treasure? What if we *don't* save the island?"

Fig frowned and rubbed her eyes. She kept her hand over her face while she answered, "We can't worry about that, Sea Hawk. Think of everything we did today—we made it through the vines, we survived the river, and we know we're supposed to go to the center of the island. We'll find the treasure."

"But if we don't," Milton persisted, "then this whole trip will be for nothing. The Culebra Company will get the island. Uncle Evan will be totally crushed. You and your mother will have to leave." He inhaled sharply, then finished with an exhale that might have literally been made of fear. "And you won't want to be my friend anymore."

Fig didn't respond for such a long time that Milton thought she had fallen back to sleep. Which was probably just as well. He didn't want to hear her say that he was right.

But then she pulled her hands from her face. The moonlight caught her wide, round eyes, and turned them into moons of their own, enormous and shining (at least to Milton's spectacle-less eyes).

"Treasure or no treasure," Fig said, "I'll still be your friend, Sea Hawk. Now go to sleep."

And after that, Milton did.

CHAPTER 48

Keep Your Fork Out

Menu-You Bush fruit was on the menu for breakfast the next morning. Milton decided his should taste like banana bread French toast. Banana bread French toast was his mother's specialty. She always made it for him on particularly difficult days, like spelling-test days, running-the-mile-in-gym-class days, returning-to-school-after-being-suspended-for-breaking-his-teacher's-nose days—that sort of thing.

Milton was pretty sure that today was going to be a difficult day. They had to finish their hike to the center of the island, find the treasure, and make it home by nightfall. Way more difficult than a spelling test.

Milton thought about his mother's banana bread French toast and took a bite of the fruit. It tasted just like it (if banana bread French toast were squishy, mushy, and juicy), and that made him feel better about the day ahead. Even though it also made him miss his mother a little.

Okay, a lot.

"Do you think your mother will notice that you didn't actually sleep in the tree ship?" he asked Fig as she disassembled the tent.

"I don't know," Fig said. She pulled the poles apart, folded the pieces together, and slid them neatly into their sack. "She trusts me, but now that it's only the two of us, she worries. I hope she doesn't check the tree ship, but I left a note saying we went hiking in the jungle in case she does."

Milton thought he could probably do what Fig was doing, so he took one of the long tent poles and lo and behold—he was able to fold it up! "My mother worries too," he said, handing Fig the pole. "She worries about a lot of things. And she works a ton too. This year especially."

"Maybe work is her *Isle of Wild*," Fig said. "I mean, the thing she does so she can be somewhere else or think about something else."

Milton considered this as he took another tent pole to fold. "I think you're probably right," he said. "I wish she could come to the Lone Island, actually. I think she'd like it here."

He had this one memory of his mother from right before the Most Totally, Terribly, Horribly, Heinously Rotten Year of All Time, when he was still in his Nature Phase. She had surprised him by coming home early and asking what he wanted to do—anything! She hadn't complained when the answer was *Backyard expedition* or even when he had lain down in a slightly muddy patch to observe the grass. She had lain down next to him.

"What's this one, Milt?" she had asked, holding up a stalk of grass.

"That," he had told her, "is Kentucky bluegrass."

"And this one?"

"Also, Kentucky bluegrass."

"And this one?"

"You found ryegrass!" Milton had cried, and his mother had laughed.

All afternoon they had examined grass and ants (from a safe distance, of course) and then (gloriously!) a cardinal. She had seemed so relaxed, not one bit impatient, and she hadn't looked at her phone or sighed even once out there under the blue sky.

"She said this summer was going to be what we all needed," he told Fig, "and I hope she's right."

After the tent was put away and the compass had been consulted, everyone shouldered their backpacks.

"Onward we go to the center of the island," Milton said as they headed out of the starry clearing.

"Keep an eye out for the Enmity-Amity Trees," Fig added. "That's our next stop."

They were deep, deep, deep in the jungle now, and it was a jungle that was growing weirder and more wonderful with every step. Rafi was taking pictures of everything (including a disproportionate number of bug shots). Gabe kept dancing ahead until Rafi called him back. Fig was as enthralled as she had been yesterday, and Milton was right there with her.

He saw trees covered in fire-truck-red fur (which seemed like a poor decision for the tropical climate, but to each their own). He saw shiny golden vines looped around and around the trees like fancy jewelry (at least he thought they were vines until the end of one turned out to have lovely black eyes and some very elegant fangs). The flowers were bigger. The colors were brighter. There were hoots and hisses above them every now and then, and Milton could have sworn some of the trees were moving.

As they hiked along, Fig read aloud from the upcoming entries, beginning with the UnderCover Cat. "*The UnderCover Cat is almost completely camouflaged,*" she read. "*The only unmirrored parts are the cat's retractable fangs, which are a foot long and razor-sharp.*"

Milton had fallen a few steps behind during this reading. He was listening, but he was also taking in the flora and fauna. Then, while he was sniffing a wispy blue-and-pink flower that smelled like cotton candy, something brushed his leg.

With a caw, Milton dropped into his self-defense pose. He was 99.99 percent sure he could maybe hear a growling sound somewhere to his left, so he reached into his backpack very slowly and found the fork he'd packed. Maybe Sea Hawk didn't harm fauna, but Milton wasn't going to be anything else's lunch. He jabbed at the air with the fork once. Twice. Thrice!

Then he ran.

"What are you doing with that fork?" Fig asked when he caught up to her. "And did you scream a minute ago?"

It took Milton a few moments before he could speak. "It was a bird-of-prey call," he gasped. "Now, don't be alarmed, because I think I handled it pretty perfectly, but I felt something touch my leg back there."

"Like a fern?" Fig asked.

"Like an UnderCover Cat," Milton said.

"Did you see the floating fangs?"

"Well, no," Milton admitted.

"Okay . . . ," Fig said. "Well, if it really was an UnderCover Cat, that's actually a good sign, Sea Hawk. The guide says the cat lives near the center of the island, so we're almost there!"

"That's all well and good, Fig," Milton replied, "but my concern is that a practically invisible feline might be stalking us right this very moment, ready to pounce and devour us whole. And I do not want to be devoured whole for a second time!"

"Keep your fork out, then," Fig said. "And let's stick together."

CHAPTER 49

Lem-Where-Aby?

Trying to regain his shaken composure, Milton put his binoculars up to his eyes and focused on the next task: finding the Enmity-Amity Trees. They had been lucky finding the Starlight Starbright Trees, but what if they weren't so lucky this time? What if they came out on the other coast by the research station, treasure-less?

He didn't have to worry. It was very clear when they'd reached their destination. Milton didn't even need his binoculars.

The Enmity-Amity Trees were exactly like the guide said—extremely tall, and riddled with hundreds of indentations. High, high up, there were blue, green, and yellow leaves, but most of the trees were composed of trunk, and rather than being round, those trunks were square.

Milton, Fig, Rafi, and Gabe kept a safe distance, because poison-thorn-shooting trees are no joke.

"So we're here," said Rafi after taking a few pictures. "What now?"

"The next entry is the SunBurst Blossoms and then the Beautimous Lemallaby," Fig said. "Maybe they're nearby, and we should trek around this area and see if we can spot them? The SunBurst Blossoms are supposed to be up high, but I think the lemallaby could be either in a tree or down in a burrow, based on their description."

After yesterday's assemblage failures and near-digestion, Milton realized this was the perfect chance to further redeem himself. He had years of birdwatching experience, after all, and this couldn't be that much different. Setting his explorer hat at a jaunty angle, he said, "Let's split into two teams. Fig and I will search up high since I have these." He brandished his neon-green binoculars, ignoring Rafi's little snort of laughter (if only he had the significantly more impressive Magnifycent2000s). "Rafi and Gabe, you search down below."

After he said this, Milton waited for Rafi to protest . . . but he didn't. He shrugged and Gabe said, "Aye, aye!" and off they went, their backs hunched as they peered around the densely foliaged jungle floor. Milton and Fig set off too, faces tilted skyward, scanning the way-up-there leaves for some sign of the massive blossoms or the monkey-possum-bandicoot-type animals.

They hiked in a circle around the trees.

No sign.

They hiked in a bigger circle.

Still no sign.

They hiked in a smaller circle again.

Not even one little sign.

After an hour of circle walking, all they had to show for it were two sore necks and two sore backs. And it turned out yesterday's truth-telling didn't guarantee eternal bliss either.

"I'm getting tired of searching for burrows that don't exist," Rafi grumbled as they rounded the Enmity-Amity Trees for the millionth time. "Any more brilliant ideas, Dr. Bird Br—"

"Watch it, Rafi," Fig cautioned.

Milton was racking his explorer hat–covered brain trying to think of what to do next. If this were *Isle of Wild*, there would be another prompt by now—a path, a creature racing by, a meowed hint from Dear Lady DeeDee. He flipped through the guide as he trudged along (which led to a lot of stumbles and stubbed toes and one spectacular face-plant), but he couldn't find any clues. So much for redeeming himself!

As the morning wore on with no further progress, Milton grew more and more discouraged. His glasses kept sliding off his sweaty nose. His backpack seemed super heavy. When he slipped for the twentieth time and hollered from the ground, "I think we should take a lunch break!" no one objected.

Milton stayed right where he was. Fig came and sat next to him. Without speaking, she handed him a bag of plantain chips and a peanut butter sandwich. He took them, but he decided to start on the jerky first. It looked pretty substantial. Maybe it would fill him up, and he could return Fig's food. He didn't want to seem like too much of a mooch.

"You know," Fig said, "that's fish jerky. Your uncle made it himself, and gave it out as a Christmas present, but we threw ours away. I'm pretty sure the Alvarezes did too. I think he ground up the whole fish, bones and all."

"At least it's not spaghetti and meatballs," Milton replied. He took a big chomp—and nearly broke his teeth. It was some seriously tough jerky.

He had switched to gnawing off little shreds when Gabe came skipping over. "Hey hey! Can I see that guide thingy?" he asked.

So far, Gabe had shown zero interest in the field guide, but Milton figured he had as much of a right to look as anyone else, so he handed it over and went back to his gnawing. Gabe sat on the ground next to him and started flipping rapidly and randomly through the cream-colored leaf-pages, humming happily.

Milton had finally managed to nibble off a chunk that did, in fact, contain quite a few bone shards when Gabe said, "Didja figure out the clue for where these wacky cats are yet?"

"A clue? For the lemallabies?" Milton asked, massaging his aching jaw.

"Yep. The one from this part: *Habitat: That's for me to know and you to find out by studying this guide from start to finish.* So didja look from start to finish yet?"

Fig and Milton exchanged a glance. "I guess we haven't done that, no," Fig told him.

"Wowzers! Well, then gimme a paper and a pen," Gabe said with a big grin. "I think I got an idea!"

CHAPTER 50

WordSmithing

Everyone gathered around to see what the youngest member of the group had figured out. He read off the first letter of every entry and had Milton copy them down in his field journal. When they finished, the letters read:

T	I	E	R	P	T	A	M
		U	E	S	B	Y	

"Tierp Tam U Esby," Fig read aloud. "You really think this is a clue, Gabe?"

"I do, I do!" Gabe sang out. "I know an anagram when I see one."

"What's an anagram?" Milton asked, squinting at the letters, which looked like gibberish to him.

"A jumble!" Gabe replied. "Letters all mixety-mixed. So I'm gonna unmix them."

"What can we do to help?" Fig asked.

"You keep schwabbin' the decks, me mateys," Gabe replied, "while I do my WordSmithing."

He took the field journal from Milton, plopped right down onto the jungle floor, and stuck his eyeballs about one inch from the letters.

"What exactly is *WordSmithing*?" Fig asked.

"The WordSmiths are a very prestigious society for the verbally gifted," Rafi explained. "Gabe's been a member since he was three. He had to take a test and everything. My dad gets about fifty newspapers in the monthly supply shipment, and he gives Gabe the word-game pages—crossword puzzles, cryptograms, jumbles."

They were quiet as Gabe studied the journal page with *TIERP-TAMUESBY* written on it. His face was screwed up, making him look more Rafi-like than usual, and he was opening and closing his mouth like a fish. Milton thought it must help him concentrate (which was fine for folks who didn't have glasses to adjust or peacock feathers to smooth).

It took almost five minutes (which doesn't seem like a long time, but when you're staring at someone who's staring at a piece of paper . . . it's a long time), but finally Gabe shouted, "Got one!" He held out his hand, and Rafi put a pencil in it.

Trees, he wrote under the letters.

"What about trees?" Fig asked.

"SHHH!" Gabe shushed. He studied his paper again. His face grew even scrunchier. He fished his lips. He cocked his head left, then right, then left again.

"It's three words," he mumbled. He held the pencil poised above the letters. Everyone else held their breath. Then he wrote:

UP AMITY TREES B

"You did it!" Rafi cried. He hugged his brother, who beamed, then flipped into a handstand.

"Toldja I was a WordSmith," he said.

"But what's the extra letter stand for?" Fig asked, eyeing Gabe's solution. "The *B*?"

"S'not extra," upside-down Gabe said. "It's what's at the top of the Enmity-Amity Trees. The entry that starts with *B*."

Milton took the field guide and flipped to the table of contents. "The *B* stands for *Beautimous Lemallaby*," he said, and with this new bit of information, it was like the pieces of Dr. Paradis's puzzle came together. "And it makes perfect sense! Remember—the field guide says the lemallabies eat SunBurst Blossoms. The Sun-

Burst Blossoms grow as high up as possible. The tallest trees are the Enmity-Amity Trees. So Little SmooshieFace and the rest of his lemallaby friends are probably at the top of these trees this very minute. We just have to climb up there!"

He let out a caw of joy. Fig grinned. Gabe (still upside down) yahooed. They knew what to do! They knew where to go!

"So we're going to climb up the three-hundred-foot-tall trees that shoot poison thorns?" Rafi asked. "Like, immediate-death-type poison thorns?"

The cawing, grinning, and yahooing stopped.

CHAPTER 51

Enmity and Amity

Staring up at one of the square, pockmarked trunks, Milton wondered how long it had taken the Enmity-Amity Trees to develop their survival adaptation of shooting poison thorns at contentious, would-be climbers. He knew that explorers and pirates and settlers and armies had been trying to make the island their own for many, many years. Had some of them wanted to hurt the lemallabies perhaps? Had they planned to harvest all the SunBurst Blossoms? Had they wanted to chop down the trees?

Whatever the Enmity-Amity Trees had been through, it was clear that they, like the Truth-Will-Out Vines, had figured out a way to protect themselves. The vines had adapted to detect lies and open only for truth-tellers. These trees had adapted to detect hostility and allow only friends to ascend.

Four friends, to be exact. If Rafi and Gabe hadn't followed them, Milton realized, he and Fig would have had to find some random Lone Island fauna to assist them like Dr. Paradis wrote about in the field guide. What a task that would have been!

. . . or maybe it would have been a hundred times easier.

A few *Restart*s would really come in handy about now.

"Listen, the guide says that we all have to touch the tree at the same time," he said, turning from the trees to his expedition mates, "one on each side of the trunk. If there's only amity between us, then the branches will pop out, and we can climb up."

"But if there's enmity," Fig said, "then this tree's super–sixth sense is going to know." She gazed pointedly at Rafi.

Rafi immediately averted his eyes. "We don't have to worry about me and Gabe," he said. "We're pretty good friends, even though he's kind of nuts."

"We're not friends!" yelled Gabe, who was scaling a big boulder next to them.

Rafi stared up at his brother. "What do you mean? Of course we are!"

"No, we're not!" Gabe insisted, his face fierce. Then, grinning, he launched himself off the rock and onto his brother. "We're best friends!" he screeched.

Rafi looked a little embarrassed, and then even more embarrassed when Gabe gave him a smooch on the top of his curly head, but he still smiled.

"That takes care of you two, then," Milton said. "And Fig and me are friends. Right, Fig? We are, aren't we?"

"You know we are, Sea Hawk," Fig replied.

Milton beamed at her. "I do indeed."

Milton's happiness only lasted for a moment though. He and Fig were amicable, and Gabe and Rafi were, but now Rafi and Fig were staring anywhere but at each other, and, truth be told, he wasn't jumping at the opportunity to hash things out with Rafi either. Gabe was just flinging sticks at the Enmity-Amity Trees and smiling expectantly at everyone.

Uncle Evan had said Dr. Paradis wanted him to go out to meet the island. Well, Milton was pretty sure that he, Fig, Rafi, and Gabe had done that. They had spoken their truths, and the vine, in turn, had shown them the true island. But it seemed to Milton that they had done quite a lot of coming out to meet one another too. They had hiked and sung and paddled and talked and watched the stars together.

Now it was time to speak truths again. If they didn't finish working out their enmity, they were going to be jabbed in the spleen.

Milton didn't want to be jabbed in the spleen. He wanted to see what was at the top of the Enmity-Amity Trees. He wanted to find the treasure. He wanted to save the island.

So he took a deep breath, adjusted his glasses, fluffed his peacock feather, and said, "Rafi, I believe there is some enmity between us. You made fruit fall on my favorite hat, you filched the field guide, and you called me names. You almost called me a name today, in fact."

Before Milton had even finished speaking, Rafi opened his mouth, as if he was ready to deny everything. Then he whipped around as one of the Enmity-Amity Trees made a decidedly sinister *FWING!*

Triggered by Gabe's stick throwing, a few holes had opened and foot-long, razor-sharp, green-tipped thorns had shot out.

They were really, really, really scary-looking.

"I know I did those things," Rafi said, eyeing the thorns. "And I know"—he turned his eyes to Milton now—"I know I wasn't exactly friendly when you first got here. I think maybe all that Triple F nature survey stuff made me feel like I had to, I don't know, prove that you weren't smarter than me. Anyway, I'm sorry."

Milton blinked his bespectacled eyes in surprise. "That is most unexpected," he said. "Prove something to *me*? You're the one with the tree ship and entomologist parents. And I'm—I'm not—" He paused. "What I mean to say is I accept your apology, and I'm sorry if I appeared to be a braggart. My intention was to befriend you."

The thought he'd had at the vines came back to him—maybe this was the time to tell everyone the truth about himself—but his stomach recoiled at the thought and he was relieved when Gabe, who was now pelting the trees with rocks, yelled, "I like you, Sea Hawk! You have a really nice hat!"

"Thank you, Gabe," Milton said. "That means a great deal to me. And I am very impressed with your WordSmithing skills."

"I like you too, Fig!" Gabe continued. "You might even know more than me."

Fig had been leaning against the boulder, watching Milton and Rafi with that jumbly expression she'd been wearing lately. "You're totally kooky," she said, "but I like you too, Gabe."

Rafi was eyeing Fig warily now. "Remember how I apologized to you yesterday?"

Fig's eyebrows went from jumbly to Maximum Arch Capacity in an instant. She shook her head, her somewhat bedraggled buns bobbing back and forth. "I do not remember that at all," she said.

"Yes, I did!" Rafi cried. "Last night. I said, *I'm sorry*. You all heard me, right?"

"That was a very unspecific apology," Milton said. "I don't think it counts."

"Me neither," Fig said, folding her arms.

"Me three-ther!" Gabe shouted, chucking a pine cone the size of a watermelon.

FWING! went the Enmity-Amity Tree.

"Okay, okay, okay," Rafi said, holding up his hands. "I meant it last night, so I can say it again. Fig, I'm sorry. I know I've been mean and stupid. But maybe we can be friends?"

As Milton watched Rafi and Fig facing each other, he thought of Fig's own words: *Everyone makes mistakes, don't they?* and he thought about how he'd hidden in video games and how Fig had hidden in books. Maybe Rafi had been hiding in prickliness and fruit throwing.

Fig didn't reply for a few seconds, and Milton was sure she'd been listening to her own words of wisdom when she finally nodded and said, "I accept your apology, Rafi. And I'm sorry for my part too."

"Does that mean there's amity between us?" Rafi asked uncertainly.

"I think so. On a temporary basis," Fig said, with the beginnings of a smile. "Let's hope the tree agrees."

They approached one of the great, holey, sky-scraping trees (Milton tiptoed because he didn't want to trip and, you know, kill everyone). They each took a side of the square trunk. Milton tried to find a hole-free space to put his hand, but there wasn't one.

If this didn't work, they would all be dead.

Some adventure!

"On the count of three," Fig said. Hands reached out. "One. Two. Three!"

225

Everyone pressed their palms to the tree trunk. Milton squeezed his eyes shut and let out a high-pitched "Eeeee!" He heard the holes click open—

And something came popping out, pushing his hand away.

But it wasn't a sharp something. Milton was intact and ungored. He cracked his eyelid (a tiny bit at first, in case there was a thorn waiting to de-eyeball him).

The Enmity-Amity Tree was covered not in thorns but in branches—hundreds of small but sturdy-looking branches up and down every side of its long trunk. Each one had five twigs sticking out of its end, like miniature wooden hands.

"Onward!" Milton yelled in victory (and serious relief). "Well, upward, actually."

It was time to talk with Little SmooshieFace.

CHAPTER 52

Tomato, Tomahto

Before coming to the Lone Island, Milton didn't think he'd ever faced a life-or-death situation outside of *Isle of Wild*. Not a single one.

Boy, had that been nice.

He'd been away from home for less than two weeks, and already he'd almost crash-landed in the ocean, almost been push-pulled into oblivion, been literally eaten, and almost gotten fanged by an invisible feline.

And now he was going to climb three hundred feet into the air with only some retractable sticks to spot him.

Milton wasn't afraid of heights, but he was most definitely afraid of falling from them. He was afraid of his entrails becoming extrails. He was afraid of becoming a Milton-shaped splatter.

Given the situation, they were reasonable fears, and he was fairly certain that everyone, even Fig the tree-climber, shared them.

They weren't going to be gouged with toxic spines (whew!), but they could still plummet to certain death (and really, tomato, tomahto. Whether you're stabbed or splattered, dead is dead).

Gabe, however, proved his hypothesis wrong.

"Here we go!" the youngest member of the group cried. Then he stuck one foot on a twig-hand and grabbed another higher up. Instead of remaining flat like little platforms, the twig-hands gripped Gabe's foot and held his hands. When he shifted to take the next step, the twig-hands assisted, pushing upward and steadying him. "Looky looky!" he called down. "Helping hands."

"Gabe, be careful! Wait for me!" Rafi yelled. He started after his brother, hollering cautions and advice.

Fig watched them, but she didn't move. She stood next to Milton while he breathed deeply and made blergh noises (fish jerky, life-or-death situations, and a very sensitive stomach were not a good combination).

"Are you ready, Sea Hawk?" Fig asked. "The lemallabies are waiting for us."

Milton adjusted his explorer hat. He straightened his glasses. "All right, Lone Island," he whispered. "We're coming up to meet you."

With Fig next to him, he started up the Enmity-Amity Tree (which was really just an Amity Tree at this point).

Shockingly, it wasn't nearly as difficult as he had imagined. Fig kept telling him that Little SmooshieFace was at the top and that they were almost there, which helped a lot. After a few dozen feet, he was practically jumping from twig-hand to twig-hand. He was scaling this tree like Sea Hawk fetching his breakfast mangoes or lunchtime guavas or nighttime coconuts. In fact, Milton didn't even notice how high he was until he was surrounded by yellow, blue, and green leaves.

It was amazing, he thought, what you could do when you had a friend by your side (and also a brawny, dashing alter ego).

The leaves at the top of the tree were long and broad and criss-crossed over one another. They formed what looked like a thatched roof over Milton's head with a small opening close to the trunk.

"Just a little higher," called Fig from below him. "Don't look down."

Milton didn't look down. He grabbed the next twig-hand, stepped up, and stuck his head through the opening.

"Great flapping falcons," he breathed. "Would you look at that."

CHAPTER 53

Close Encounters of the Furred Kind

Here, at the tippy top of the canopy, the leaves formed a blue, green, and yellow floor. These thick and fibrous leaves were laced together so tightly that Rafi and Gabe were standing on them. Taller Enmity-Amity Trees towered above, like pillars holding up the very blue sky.

Further beautifying this aerial-arboreal enclave were enormous, brilliantly hued flowers that clung to the tree trunks and burst out of the leaf-floor. These flowers came in every color— mustard yellow and cornflower blue, ochre and puce, coral and alabaster—and Milton knew exactly what they were: SunBurst Blossoms! The blossoms were in full bloom, and they smelled good enough to eat.

And they were definitely being eaten. Because perched up and down and all around were pointy-eared, round-eyed, bushy-tailed animals about the size of large house cats. About the size, Milton realized with a gasp, of Dear Lady DeeDee.

The animals were not paying the slightest bit of attention to the newcomers. They were too busy shoving SunBurst Blossom after SunBurst Blossom into their bucktoothed mouths. They had mostly greenish-bluish-yellowish fur, like the leaves of the Enmity-Amity Tree—except for their hairy tushies.

Each booty featured a SunBurst Blossom pattern.

There was no doubt about it—they had found the Beautimous Lemallabies!

There was no cawing, grinning, or yahooing, however.

Instead, everyone huddled near the tree hole, wary-eyed and motionless. Because the facts were these: They were surrounded by a large group of wild animals. Animals with shiny, sharp teeth. Animals with alarmingly long claws.

Milton wasn't *scared* (Sea Hawk was *never* scared, not even while he was being eaten), but he didn't know if it was wise to move too quickly (or maybe at all . . . ever).

Then he heard a high-pitched giggle. Next to him, Rafi gasped.

"Gabe," he hissed. "Don't make any sudden movements. I'm coming to get you."

Gabe had skipped across the springy leaf-floor and plopped down with a group of lemallabies. Two of them skittered close and began combing through his curly hair. Occasionally, one would

231

pluck something out and pop it into its mouth. A smaller lemallaby with a chartreuse booty climbed into Gabe's lap. Another brought him a periwinkle blossom.

"These wacky monkeys like me!" Gabe cried.

Rafi let out a long, quavering sigh. "That's because you never, ever shower," he replied as the lemallabies continued grooming Gabe. "And they're not monkeys. They're Bottomy Wallabies."

"They're Beautimous Lemallabies," Milton said. "And they are truly beautimous."

Now that Gabe had paved the way, Milton decided it was time to make his move. Whenever Sea Hawk met a new creature, he approached it as if he were a member of its species. He slithered toward snakes. He hopped toward kangaroos. He curled up in a ball and somersaulted toward pangolins. In the opening story of *Isle of Wild*, he crawled toward Dear Lady DeeDee, meowing his heart out.

So Milton got down on his hands and knees. He scampered (to the best of his ability) over to Gabe and his circle of furry friends, where he tried to mimic the chittering vocalizations that the lime-green-bottomed lemallaby nearest him was making.

The lemallaby gave him a side-eye glance and edged away.

But as soon as he sat quietly back on his haunches and removed his hat, that side-eye-giving lemallaby skittered over and started picking through his hair.

"I think they like me!" Milton cried.

CHAPTER 54

Little SmooshieFace

While Milton and Gabe stayed with the lemallabies, Fig went to get a closer look at the SunBurst Blossoms, and Rafi snapped pictures.

"Shouldn't we ask them about Little SmooshieFace?" Fig said after watching a few minutes of the debugging with a slightly unsettled look on her face.

"I shall do it," Milton replied. He rose to his feet slowly so as not to upset his animal companions.

Milton had always wanted a Dear Lady DeeDee—a faithful friend who would ride on his shoulder, speak to him in a secret language, and love him unconditionally. Now he was only seconds away from having exactly that. Feet planted on the leaf-floor and Sea Hawkian bravery coursing through him, Milton turned to address the lemallabies.

"Greetings to you, Beautimous Lemallabies!" he cried. "We have come seeking Little SmooshieFace."

In response, lemallabies all over the canopy started making a honky-snorty kind of noise. It sounded like they had terrible head colds.

"Is Little SmooshieFace here?" Milton asked.

The honk-snorts grew louder. The lemallabies started elbowing one another and grinning bucktoothed grins.

"Can you ask Little SmooshieFace to come out?" Milton tried again.

Now the lemallabies were rolling on the blue-green-yellow leaf-floor. They were falling out of the branches they were perched on. They were, Milton realized, in hysterics about something. He glanced over at Fig, who shrugged in bemusement.

What was so funny about Little SmooshieFace?

He was about to ask after Dr. Paradis's favorite lemallaby for a fourth time when he saw one of the marsupial-rodent-primate creatures making his way across the treetop clearing. This lemallaby stood out to Milton because he wasn't laughing. He was smaller than the others, but he must have been old since his face fur was gray. He moved with resigned weariness, his eyes averted from his treemates.

On his booty was a teal SunBurst Blossom pattern.

"I know that bottom!" Milton cried (which was something he

had never had the opportunity to say before). "You're the Milton Macaw! Well, that's what I thought you were when I saw you by Dr. Paradis's house." His eyes widened behind his glasses. "You led me to the field guide!"

The lemallaby held out his paw, and Milton shook it.

"You're Little SmooshieFace?" he asked.

The other lemallabies broke into hysterics yet again.

Little SmooshieFace let his head fall in a nod, then kept it hanging low.

Fig came to stand by Milton and the teal-bootied lemallaby. "What's wrong, Little SmooshieFace?" she asked.

Now the lemallabies had formed a circle around them. They were snorting and snickering and howling. Glancing around, Milton had an unpleasant sense of déjà vu.

And he realized, suddenly, what they were laughing about.

Little SmooshieFace was the Bird Brain of the lemallabies.

Milton didn't know if he could fix that entirely, but he did know something that might help, at least temporarily.

"If I may ask," he said, "did Dr. Paradis select your name?"

Little SmooshieFace nodded once.

"And I'm guessing that's not the name you would have chosen for yourself?"

Little SmooshieFace peeked up at Milton, then gazed back down at the leaf-floor. He shook his head.

235

Around the Enmity-Amity Tree canopy, the lemallabies were leaning in like they couldn't wait for another chance to break into laughter. So Milton knelt next to Little SmooshieFace. He got very close to him, right up to his furry ear. "I know about that," he whispered. "How about we think of a new name for you?"

Little SmooshieFace studied Milton's bespectacled eyes for a moment, then let out a soft, approving chitter.

"How about Wally?" Milton suggested. "Wally the Lemallaby?"

Little SmooshieFace let out a chitter that was significantly less approving and wrinkled his cute little nose.

"Sunny?"

Another nose-wrinkle.

"Teal-Tushie?"

Little SmooshieFace bared his oversize front teeth and growled.

Milton held up his hands. "No Teal-Tushie," he said. "Got it. Maybe something a little . . . bolder?"

Little SmooshieFace nodded so hard his ears flapped.

Milton tugged his explorer hat down low as he thought. This new name had to be fierce, wild, and totally awesome. "How about Lord . . . um . . . Snarlsy?"

Little SmooshieFace's eyes widened in his (really super adorable) face. He gave a bucktoothed grin, then snarled his approval.

"Mighty moles and voles!" Milton cried, striking a self-defense pose. "What a ferocious lemallaby this is! Little, perhaps, but definitely not smooshie in the least. No, no. I shall call him Lord Snarlsy, which I think is actually his real name."

Every fuzzy mouth dropped open in surprise as the lemallaby formerly known as Little SmooshieFace leaped into the air and began vine-swinging his way around the canopy. Lord Snarlsy snarled and hooted. He beat his chest like a gorilla. He wagged his floral behind at his treemates. It probably wasn't the response that Milton would have advised, but he let the teal-tushied lemallaby go for a pretty long time before gesturing for him to come back down.

Milton knew what it felt like to be given a name, after all.

And he knew what it felt like to choose a new one.

"I'm glad we settled that," he said when the lemallaby, panting and bright-eyed, was next to him again. "Now, Lord Snarlsy, you must know why we're here." He pulled the field guide out of his zippered pocket and held it out.

Lord Snarlsy reached out his very humanlike hands and took the leaf-pages. He flipped through them, stopping on the *Beautimous Lemallaby* entry. The illustration there was of a small, shy-looking lemallaby: Lord Snarlsy himself.

Fig, who had taken a few steps back during the renaming saga, reapproached them. "The island is in danger," she said. "Dr. Paradis wrote that you would be the one to ask questions if that ever happened. We need to find her treasure."

Lord Snarlsy turned one more leaf-page, then studied the illustration there. It was the final entry, the Yes-No-Maybe-So Tree.

"Will you help us?" Fig asked.

The lemallaby looked up from the field guide. He met Fig's eyes, then Milton's. He glanced over at Rafi, who had been gawking at him since his vine-swinging performance, and at Gabe, who was practicing his own vine-swinging.

Then he dropped the guide and leaped through the tree-trunk opening.

CHAPTER 55

Follow the Leader

Milton let out a yelp of horror.

He dashed across the yellow-blue-green leaf-floor, but then hesitated. He didn't want to look down the Enmity-Amity Tree trunk and see the lemallaby-shaped splatter at the bottom.

When he finally steeled his stomach and peeked over the edge, however, there was no Lord Snarlsy splatter to be seen. Instead, he saw the lemallaby skittering down the tree trunk, then flinging himself into a nearby neon-pink palm. He paused there, waving up at Milton from his perch.

"Time to go," Milton said to Fig, Rafi, and Gabe.

They touched the tree trunk again (it was slightly less terrifying the second time around), and the twig-hands popped out. On the way down, the twig-hands lowered them from branch to branch.

Milton was hardly even scared (he only screamed seven times . . . maybe eight).

As soon as they reached the ground, Lord Snarlsy leaped from his palm to a shrub with spiraling branches and seedpods shaped like tiny bells.

"Do you want us to follow you?" Fig called up to Lord Snarlsy. He nodded, setting the seedpod-bells to ringing, then scampered along the twisty branches and launched himself onward.

Across the jungle they went, with Lord Snarlsy pausing every few yards to wait. Never once did the lemallaby's feet touch the ground as he led them past a few Sweet Pickle Trees, through a maze of bristly bushes that were filled with birds' nests (unoccupied, thank heaven, since Milton suspected they belonged to Tone-Deaf Warblers) and behind a line of pine-like shrubs that had sparkly pompoms instead of needles.

Then they came to an impossibly tall waterfall. The water wasn't the muddy brown of the river they'd canoed in, but a bright, clear turquoise, and rainbows sparkled in the mist all around. On the far side of the waterfall, there was a clump of Truth-Will-Out Vine, and Lord Snarlsy flung himself right onto the strands. Hanging there, he chattered something in Lemallabese. Milton wondered what kind of truths a monkey-marsupial-ferret would have (*I ate the last magenta SunBurst Blossom*, or maybe *It was me who threw poop at the Astari Night Avis last night*).

Whatever he said, the vines listened. They parted to reveal a path that led behind the waterfall—a path that Lord Snarlsy swung through.

Milton, Fig, Rafi, and Gabe raced after him.

When they came out on the other side, they were in a clearing that Milton felt quite certain was the most beautiful place he'd ever seen—on-screen or in person. The ground was covered in thick, vibrantly green moss. The tree trunks were pure white with jewel-toned leaves that met high above, forming a floral dome. The light filtering through this many-hued canopy was tinted with color and aswirl with gold-shimmering insects, their wings emitting a gentle *shhh*.

It wasn't just the way the clearing *looked* that made it beautiful though. From the moment he came through the vines, Milton felt it—that same feeling he used to get on his backyard expeditions, the feeling that had come back to him this summer, the feeling he could only find when he went out to meet the world around him.

Milton felt like he was as alive as he'd ever been in this full-of-life place, the center of the Lone Island.

CHAPTER 56

Yes, No, Maybe So

For quite a while, the four stood silent and still in the clearing, watching the flight of the golden insects (the least gross bugs Milton had ever seen by far) and gazing up at the collage of leaf-light above.

Then Lord Snarlsy broke the spell with a string of chattered Lemallabese.

He was perched on the branch of a tree in the center of the clearing. The tree had a black trunk and dozens of black branches. The branches were crowded with leaves that were rectangular and cream colored and very familiar, and seedpods that were long, thin, and pointed.

It was, of course, the Yes-No-Maybe-So Tree.

From his branch, Lord Snarlsy nodded at Milton, Fig, Rafi, and Gabe. He nodded, and then he shook his head. He pointed at the trunk. He jumped up and down on the branches so that the leaves waved around.

It was very clear that the lemallaby wanted them to do something. But what?

"Are we climbing this tree too?" Gabe asked. "I can climb it!"

"I don't think so," Milton said. "The Yes-No-Maybe-So Tree is the final entry in the field guide. What do we know about it, Fig?"

Fig took the field guide out and turned to the last page. "I think this is the most important part," she said after a moment. "*The Yes-No-Maybe-So Tree will also answer any question—although it can only respond (you guessed it)* Yes, No, *or* Maybe So. *By now, I'm sure you can think of a few questions to ask, can't you?*"

"Let's ask it about the treasure," Rafi said. He marched up to the tree, cupped his hands around his mouth, and yelled, "Hey, tree, we have some questions for you! Are you ready?"

The tree didn't answer. Crouched above them, Lord Snarlsy gave a snort of laughter, then covered his mouth in apology.

"Yes-No-Maybe-So Tree," Fig tried, "would you be willing to speak with us, please?"

The tree still didn't answer. *Shhh* went the insect wings.

Fig studied the entry again, while Milton peered over her shoulder. If there was one thing he had learned over and over, it was the value of consulting the field guide (even when he didn't want to). Dr. Paradis hadn't made this expedition easy. She hadn't handed them answers or shortcuts, but so far, she had always given them just enough. There had to be another clue here.

But no matter how many times he read or reread the entry, he couldn't find one in the words, and the illustration showed the tree exactly the same as it appeared in front of them.

Exactly the same, Milton noticed suddenly, except that on its leaves were black scribbles.

"Mighty moles and voles!" Milton cried. "Trees can't speak!"

"Seriously, Sea Hawk?" Fig said. "I think we've definitely figured out that anything on the Lone Island can do—well, anything."

Rafi understood what Milton really meant. "The tree doesn't have a mouth or ears," he said. "It has pages and pens."

"You gotta write a letter," Gabe said. He skipped over to the tree and tugged down a leaf-page, then unwound a seedpod stem from one of the black branches. "Here!"

Fig gave Milton the field guide and hurried over to take the seedpod pen and the leaf-page. "Okay," she said. "What should we write?"

"Ask where the treasure is," Milton suggested.

Fig read aloud as she wrote on the leaf-page:

"Do you know where Dr. Paradis's treasure is hidden?"

Right away, the sap-ink question began to shift and new letters formed. They were flowy, curlicue letters. The tree had very nice penmanship. It wrote:

YES.

"It knows!" Fig cried. She tilted the leaf so everyone could see the reply. "What should I ask now?"

"Ask where it is!" Gabe shouted.

"Yes or no questions only," Fig reminded them. "How about, *Is the treasure nearby?*" She wrote, waited a moment, then held up the leaf: *MAYBE SO.*

"Come on, you kooky tree." Fig sighed. "What do we do now?"

Holding the field guide between them, Rafi and Milton both read the entry yet again. "What's this part?" Rafi asked, pointing to the last line. "*Food Source: Mostly sunshine but the tree may ingest—and possibly regurgitate—the occasional stacks of paper-leaves and more.* What's that supposed to mean?"

Milton shuddered. Having been regurgitated in the not-so-distant past, he preferred not to dwell on this section of the entry. "I guess it can eat itself," he said. "Blergh."

Fig was tapping her chin thoughtfully with the seedpod pen. "I think Rafi's onto something," she said. "It says *stacks* of leaf-pages. Leaves don't fall in stacks. What if someone stacked them and put them in the tree?"

"Maybe Dr. Paradis fed the tree a treasure map!" Gabe cried. He held up a leaf on which he had drawn a winding line ending in an *X.* "What say you, me mateys?"

"Could be, Gabe," Rafi said, then turned to Fig. "Can I try something?"

Fig held out the leaf-page and seedpod.

Rafi took them and scrawled a new question, reading it out loud: *"Could you spit out those leaf-pages?"*

The tree did not answer. No letters appeared on any of its leaves. Milton wondered if it had run out of ink. Or maybe it wasn't in the mood to chat. Lord Snarlsy watched, his arms and tail now wrapped tightly around the branch he was perched on.

Suddenly, the tree began to move.

Roots shifted, sending Fig and Rafi stumbling backward. Limbs began to wriggle and shake. The tree was like someone trying to get change out of the pockets of too-tight pants. It twisted and shivered and stretched, and then there was a creaky-groany sound and—

A hole opened up at the tree's base.

Milton raced forward and, after a moment of hesitation, shoved his hand in. He felt the rough edges of the hole and a few spider-webs (which almost made him yank his hand back out, but he persevered!), and then his fingers brushed something thick and papery and something scratchy and bulky. Straining forward as far as he could, he reached in with both hands, grabbed, and pulled.

And there it was, the treasure of the Lone Island, out in the sunlight at last.

CHAPTER 57

Treasure!

The treasure was not one thing but two. The largest item was a satchel that was almost the size of Fig's hiking pack. It appeared to be made of woven Enmity-Amity leaves, and it was so heavy that Milton dropped it onto the mossy ground right away.

The other item was a book. The book was made of Yes-No-Maybe-So leaf-pages and tightly bound in Truth-Will-Out Vine, like the guide that had led them there. Instead of being a thin stack, however, this book was hundreds of pages long.

"*The COMPLETE Lone Island Field Guide*." Milton read the title aloud. "*By Dr. Ada Paradis.*"

That was as far as Milton got because then Fig was there next to him. He handed the book over. He wanted her to be the first one to see what was inside.

With everyone watching, Fig opened the book. Her eyes grew

impossibly large as she read what was written there and then began to flip through the pages, one after another, faster and faster. Milton started to wonder if perhaps she was planning on perusing the entire massive tome before giving them some answers, when she burst out, "Do you realize what this is?"

"That's what we're waiting for you to tell us," Rafi said. "Is it another field guide or what?"

Fig shook her head, then nodded it, then shook it again. "Yes!" she cried. "But look." She hoisted the book up in both hands. "The Prince-Frog, Orange-You-Glad Orangutan, Combustible Gerbil, Luminescent Liana, Silliest Goose, DoorWay Tree, Indescribably Weird Thingamabob." She turned the pages, showing them the detailed illustrations and lengthy entries for each. "There are hundreds of plants and animals in here. Maybe thousands!"

"It's the whole Lone Island!" yelped Gabe. "In a book."

"It really is," Fig said. "And it's way more detailed than the original field guide. Detailed enough, I think, to be the proof we need—proof that this island is bursting with brand-new species and should be protected at all costs." She hugged the enormous tome to herself. "Which means . . . we did it!"

She let out a shout of joy and spun around in a circle. Milton threw his magnificent hat high in the air and birdcalled his own excitement. Rafi and Gabe high-fived and hugged. Finally—finallly!—they had found the treasure. They had saved the island!

They all gathered around Fig to take a closer look at the new guide. Pictured on the first page was none other than their favorite Beautimous Lemallaby, Lord Snarlsy, but this entry contained far more information than the one in their original guide, complete with a suggested Latin name (*Lemallabus dulcis*).

"I would probably be the most famous naturalist in history if I turned this in as my nature survey," Milton remarked, tapping the smooshie-faced illustration.

"Seriously, Sea Hawk?" Fig said.

"Hypothetically, of course," Milton assured her. "This treasure is for island-saving purposes only." He poked the leaf-bag with one hiking-booted toe. "What about the bag?"

Rafi knelt down and started to untie the vine, then paused. Attached was a small leaf-card with a message written on it. "*No species were harmed in the collection of these samples,*" he read aloud.

Then he stuck his hand into the bag and pulled out—

A skull!

Not a human one (thank goodness!). Not a lemallaby one either. The skull was the size of Rafi's fist, with two large canine teeth and a tag that read, *Three-Eyed Sloth: Bradypus tri-oculi.*

"Yowzers," Gabe breathed. "Is the whole bag full of bones?"

Carefully, Rafi and Fig emptied the satchel, laying its contents out on the ground. There *were* more bones, each labeled, but there was much more. There were flowers and leaves, carefully pressed and stored in wooden boxes. There were fossils and shells and the molted exoskeletons of insects (so gross). There were jars and bags and leaf-page envelopes, each containing samples.

"Look at all this treasure," Milton said, gazing around.

"Environmental groups and scientists around the world will support Dr. Greene if they see this," Fig said.

"Plus we have Lord Snarlsy in the flesh," Milton added. "Everyone loves cute, little"—he paused and glanced over at the lemallaby, who was baring his (alarmingly sharp) front teeth—"er, I mean, fierce wild animals."

"Whoa!" Rafi suddenly started dumping the samples back into the satchel. "Give me that," he said, snatching the foot-long talon that Gabe had been using to pick his nose.

"Whadaya doing?" Gabe asked, replacing the talon with a finger.

"We haven't been watching the time," Rafi said. "The sun sets in about four hours, and we're still a long way from home. If we don't leave now, we won't make it back before dark."

CHAPTER 58

Bye-Bye

Milton could hardly believe it, but Rafi was right. Somehow the time had gotten away from them. Fig set about transferring some of her gear to Rafi's and Gabe's bags so that she could fit the new guide and the satchel in her pack, while Milton turned to Lord Snarlsy, who had remained on his perch throughout the treasure-related proceedings.

"Lord Snarlsy, are you ready?" Milton called up to him. "The time has come for us to go onward."

With a big bucktoothed smile, the lemallaby pointed up to the sky, then waved his paw in an unmistakable gesture: *Bye-bye.*

"Not bye-bye," Milton said, laughing at his (totally adorable) new companion. "We want you to come along."

Lord Snarlsy cocked his head to one side. Then he pointed

upward, more insistently this time, and waved his paw again: *Bye-bye.*

"My good Lord," Milton tried again, "this guide and the samples are extraordinary, but so are you. You're a whole new class of animal! Please do us the honor of accompanying us back to the beach. I'll even let you ride on my shoulder for some of the time."

Lord Snarlsy flung himself from the midnight-black branch and into one of the white-limbed trees nearby. He waved over his shoulder:

Bye-bye.

"Lord Snarlsy, wait!" Milton cried, racing along the ground after his much-longed-for fauna friend. "We need you! Dr. Paradis wanted you to help us."

Lord Snarlsy paused when he heard Dr. Paradis's name, then leaped onto Milton's shoulder (which was heavenly . . . although a tad heavy). Chattering a few sentences in Lemallabese, the furry creature pointed up at the sky, then at the watch hanging from Milton's utility belt, then spread his arms wide, like he was hugging a big crowd of friends. Milton nodded along—although he had no idea what was going on.

Then Lord Snarlsy pointed to his eyeballs, waved bye-bye one last time, and, before Milton could say, *Nooooooo!* leaped away and skittered back up the white tree to the rainbow-leafed dome above—where he disappeared from view.

"Nooooooo!" Milton cried, hand outstretched.

"Get him!" Rafi hollered. He started to shimmy up one of the pale trunks, but stopped after a few feet.

There were no noises above them. There was no sign of the teal-tushied lemallaby.

He was gone.

"We have to go back to the Enmity-Amity Trees!" Milton cried, whirling toward the secret waterfall passage. "We have to convince him to come with us!"

But Fig, shouldering her treasure-filled pack, shook her head.

"We don't even know if that's where he went," she said, "and if he doesn't want to come with us, we don't have time to chase him down. The guide and the samples are more than enough. It's time to go home."

CHAPTER 59

Homeward Bound

The hike through the dense jungle didn't take nearly as long now that they knew where they were going. Even so, it was after five o'clock by the time they reached the river, and Fig figured they had at least four more hours of hiking to go. Because the Lone Island was near the equator, days were about twelve hours long, even in the summer, and darkness fell quickly after sunsets.

So they had four more hours of hiking left. And less than two hours of light.

"We can't spend another night out here," Rafi said. "I told my parents I'd have Gabe back. They're going to freak out!"

"Plus, who knows what Uncle Evan's going to do," Milton added, pushing aside foliage and leaping over underbrush as fast as he could. "He said he had until Friday to turn in any final research to the court or sign papers saying he gives up. What if he decides to give up?"

"There is a way to get back faster," Fig said.

"Find a flock of Astari Night Avis and have them fly us home in their talons!" Gabe cried.

"Not exactly." Fig pointed downstream. There on the riverbank, right where they'd left them, were the red and yellow canoes. "I know none of us were planning on getting back on that river, but the tide is going out, so the current is in our favor. If we paddle fast, we might be able to make it to the bay before sunset."

Milton had a five-second, out-of-body flashback to the Push-Pull Centopus rising out of the water and himself huddled at the bottom of the sinking vessel, and It. Was. Terrifying. No, he did not like Fig's idea one bit. Another night in the jungle probably wouldn't *kill* them, but the centopus almost certainly would.

He was caught more than a little off guard when Rafi said, "Sea Hawk and I can handle the centopus," and thumped him on the back so hard that he dropped to his knees on the muddy bank. "Sorry, Sea Hawk," Rafi said, helping Milton to his feet.

Milton wasn't so sure they could handle it. He wasn't sure he, personally, could handle seeing the hundred legs of the Push-Pull Centopus writhing around in the water again, spewing river water like an evil-firehose monster.

But Rafi was smiling at him, and Fig was right: The river was their best option. Their only option, really.

"Indeed we can. I suppose. Perhaps," Milton said. "Yes. I'm ready." He sang a discordant octave to warm up.

"Save that for the centopus," Fig said, holding her hands over her ears.

Everyone grabbed a paddle except Milton. Fig was willing to put up with Milton's singing in order to save her life, but not his paddling. Milton put the original field guide in his dry bag, along with his HandHeld. Fig double-checked the guide and satchel in her pack, then tucked it safely under her seat, while Rafi put away his camera. After he and Gabe were buckled into their life vests, they all helped pull the canoes into the water, and off they went.

With the tide pushing them along, they were soon speeding down the river. The sky was blue, the sun was warm, they had incontrovertible proof that the island was spectacularly worth conserving, and home was only a few hours away. Everyone was feeling good, even Milton, who viewed Lord Snarlsy's leaving as a personal betrayal (that fickle lemallaby was no Dear Lady DeeDee, that was for sure).

Yes, indeed, there were two boats full of happiness on the river.

Until something struck the side of the red canoe with a *splat*.

Milton tumbled right off his seat. When he pulled himself up and leaned over the edge of the canoe, he saw that the water had begun to churn and bubble. Waves were building.

"Not again," he groaned.

Water rolled forward and crashed into the canoes, hard. The front end of each lifted into the air, then smashed back down.

"Showtime, guys!" Fig yelled, paddling with all her might.

Milton glanced across to the yellow canoe, ready to coordinate this performance in spite of the fact that liquefied panic was now pulsing through his veins. Rafi, however, was not ready. He was goggle-eyed, rigid, and . . . totally silent.

It seemed he had overestimated his ability to *handle* the centopus.

There was nothing else for it. It was up to the boy formerly known as Milton P. Greene to take the lead.

"*Great green gobs of greasy, grimy gopher guts!*" Milton belted out, rising unsteadily to his feet.

That was as far as he got.

Because the centopus's body was underwater.

It couldn't hear a single tone-deaf note.

Before Milton could sing the next line of his glorious serenade (*mutilated monkey meat*), there was a sound like a fish slapping a gong, and the front of the red canoe was launched out of the water.

Milton was launched with it.

There was a weightless, surreal moment when he thought he might not fall into the water but might somehow keep flying. Maybe he had acquired superpowers! Even Sea Hawk couldn't fly.

Then he belly-flopped into the river.

257

Spluttering and spewing water like a quadopus, Milton resurfaced in the tentacley-tempest-tossed river. Frothy whitecaps surrounded him, and slimy somethings kept slithering around his legs. A flash of teal above distracted him momentarily, but then he spotted his backpack bobbing nearby. He started to dog paddle toward it, but he kept getting knocked under the waves and firehosed in the face.

If it wasn't for the ginormous tidal wave that broke over his head, tumbled him up and over, and finally deposited him and his backpack on the riverbank, Milton would have been a goner.

Once he'd taken a few gasping breaths, he lifted his head from the mud. Downriver, Gabe was crawling out of the water, and Rafi was close behind him, both of them in their life vests.

But Fig wasn't on the riverbank.

Fig was still in the water with the Push-Pull Centopus.

CHAPTER 60

Saved, You Kook

Fig was in the middle of the river. And she wasn't swimming toward the riverbank. She kept coming up, taking gulps of air, and then diving back down again.

"Fig!" Milton cried when she surfaced the next time. "Get out of there! That centopus is going to sucker punch you into an oblivion!"

Fig didn't listen. She inhaled and went under again.

Meanwhile, the centopus seemed to be getting more and more furious by the second. Its water-engorged body was still underwater, but it was flinging its tentacles willy-nilly, banging into the now-empty canoes and spewing water to the high heavens.

When Fig resurfaced, she was even closer to the epicenter of the frothing madness. Too close—one of the tentacles smacked her in the head. She would have been all right (it was a hard hit but tentacles are quite squishy), but the sucker fastened onto her forehead.

Then another sucker got her on the arm and another on the neck. She tried to twist away, but those suckers held tight.

Fig was stuck!

Before he even had time to wonder what Sea Hawk would do, Milton P. Greene was off.

He dove (belly first) into the river and began swimming as fast as his not-exactly-brawny limbs would take him toward Fig and the Push-Pull Centopus.

Fig was putting up a fierce fight. She was treading water with her legs while trying to pry the suckers from her skin with one hand and whack any nearby tentacles with the other. She wasn't having much success though. The suckers weren't unsucking, and the tentacles kept coming.

"What are you doing, you kook?" she yelled as Milton dog paddled up. "Go back, Sea Hawk!"

But he swam on, while fumbling one handedly with the snaps of his utility belt until he found what he was searching for.

His air horn.

Milton wasn't sure what kind of noise a submerged air horn made, but he was pretty sure it wasn't melodious.

Ducking beneath the waves, he aimed the horn at the centopus and pulled the trigger. Hundreds of bubbles came shooting out. At the same time, he did his best to belt out an underwater song. It was muffley and muted and gargley, but it was most definitely tone-deaf.

Instantly, the roiling river stilled. Suckers ceased their sucking, releasing Fig with a squelchy sigh. Tentacles retracted, waving so long as they drifted down, down. The creature's water-filled body deflated and sank to the bottom of the river—to sleep, perchance to dream about whatever Push-Pull Centopuses dream about (a world where centopus-warbler love is possible?).

Milton, resurfacing into the sunshine, cawed in triumph. He had done it! He had saved Fig.

But now that he had, now that adrenaline and terror weren't fueling him, he was suddenly acutely aware of how exhausted he was. He could only dog paddle for so long. His arms and legs weren't working together anymore. They weren't really working at all, in fact. The current was starting to drag him, but it wasn't taking him to the shore this time.

Sea Hawk's near-death cry came to him again: *Shall Sea Hawk perish thus?* When he was playing *Isle of Wild*, Milton always responded to this cry with increased button-pressing and joystick-jiggling. In the water now, he was trying to save himself, but there were no buttons and no joystick. There was only water and current and fear.

Then something grabbed him around the waist.

For a second, he thought the centopus had returned. Then he heard a voice, the voice he had come to love best of all that summer, a voice that meant business right now. "Come on, Sea Hawk! Just kick and we'll get out of this river together."

261

"Fig!" Milton sputtered. "I thought I was going to drown. We still might drown! I don't have a lot of upper-body strength. I don't have a lot of lower-body strength either. We should—"

"Seriously, Sea Hawk? Stop talking," Fig ordered. "Just kick."

Milton shut his mouth and kicked with as much umph as he could muster. Fig swam forward while keeping one arm around Milton, pulling him along. She didn't let go or pause once.

Finally, they reached the shore.

Milton flopped down into the mud. "You saved me," he told Fig as she collapsed next to him.

"*You* saved *me*, you kook," Fig replied. She was covered in huge welts from the suckers, her hair buns had come unraveled, and her eyes were positively enormous. But she was smiling at him.

"We saved each other," Milton said.

Fig nodded. "We did."

CHAPTER 61

Nonetheless

From downriver, Rafi and Gabe came squelching over at top speed.

"Wowzers!" Gabe shouted, throwing himself down next to Milton. "You almost got sucked up and spewed out."

Rafi stood over them, wide eyes flicking from Sea Hawk to Fig and back like he couldn't believe they were still in one piece. "You're okay?" he said. "You're both really okay?" He shook his head. "I can't believe I froze up like that."

"It's quite all right," said Milton, still flat on his back. "I mean, we're quite all right. A tad winded, perhaps."

Fig struggled to sit up. "I have to tell you all something," she said.

Her usually strong and steady voice was wobbly, and when Milton propped himself up on his elbows, he saw that her eyes were now gleaming and unblinking. He had never seen her look like that, not even when she talked about her father.

"Fig," he said. "What's wrong?"

Fig took a shaky breath. "I—I lost my backpack," she said. "That's why I didn't swim to shore. I was trying to find it in the water. The samples are gone. And the"—her voice cracked—"the complete field guide is gone."

Rafi jumped up and started splashing into the water. "We'll find it!" he said.

As if in reply, a tentacle came snaking out of the water and spewed a fountain toward the riverbank.

"It's not safe," Fig said as Rafi yelped and leaped back. "And we won't make it home by nightfall if we don't get moving now, and if we don't make it home then Dr. Greene might sign those papers giving up the island." Fig wrapped her arms around her legs and let her face fall onto her knees. "Not that it matters anyway since I lost the treasure. I ruined everything."

Fig started to cry.

Milton lowered his head back onto the mud. The glorious blue of the sky above during this dark and dismal moment seemed as discordant as the song of a Tone-Deaf Warbler. They had traveled so far. They had risked so much. They had come out to meet the island, and the island had come out to meet them. And now the treasure was river detritus, floating downstream toward the great, swallowing deep.

They weren't going to save the island. It was over.

Milton started to cry too.

He lay in the mud on the shores of a river halfway around the world from his home, and he cried. He cried because it had been a rotten year, the worst he'd ever had. He cried because he'd thought the rottenness was over but . . . it wasn't.

Maybe no matter what he did—change his name, move to a practically deserted island, unearth hidden treasure—maybe spectaculousness was always going to be out of reach for him. Maybe he was going to have the Most Totally, Terribly, Horribly, Heinously Rotten *Life* of All Time.

But then Milton turned his head, and he saw Fig's shoulders shaking, and he heard her gasping sobs, and his heart felt like it was being squeezed and wrung out, but then filled back up again. Over and over.

The year had been rotten. Losing the field guide was rotten.

But the spectaculous had happened, nonetheless.

Fig had happened.

And this island had happened. This island, with its truth-detecting vines and knowledge-giving trees and super-alive-right-here feeling.

Maybe on one hand, it didn't seem like much had really changed for Milton P. Greene. He was sprawled out in the muck, and he had failed once again. But on the other hand, Milton P. Greene himself had changed. He knew he had.

He didn't feel like Sea Hawk. He didn't feel like Bird Brain. He felt somewhere in between, and that somewhere-in-between Milton wasn't going to give up.

"We can still do it," he said quietly. "We can still save the island."

Fig inhaled shakily and rubbed her eyes on her sleeves. "What do you mean?" she said. "No, we can't."

"We can," Milton said, struggling to sit up. "We can tell Uncle Evan about Lord Snarlsy and everything we saw. We can convince him to ask the courts for more time."

"I can show him this hairball one of those wacky monkey cats gave me," Gabe offered. He held up a wet clump of yellow-blue-green fur.

"Indeed, you can," Milton said. "We've made it this far, and I, for one, am not going to abandon this expedition when we're so close to the end."

He rose to his feet, puffed out his vest-covered chest, adjusted his sopping wet peacock feather, and pointed one sludge-covered finger up to that glorious blue sky.

"The adventure isn't over! The adventure is now!"

CHAPTER 62

The Truth of the Matter

In Milton's mind, this declaration should have been met with three cheers and a standing ovation. It had been (in his opinion) extremely inspirational.

Gabe's reaction was satisfactory. He shouted, "Aye, aye, captain, my captain!" and did a celebratory somersault through the mud.

But Rafi only said, "I hope so, Sea Hawk," and Fig just gave a weary nod. When she rose to her feet, she moved like she was still weighed down by her now-lost-at-sea backpack.

Milton tried not to take it personally. He shouldered his pack and as they set out, he led the way.

Well, he led the way for about five minutes. He had zero idea where they were, and his whole body felt like it was filled with slime instead of bones and muscles, so he contented himself with bringing up the rear on the much subdued and very damp trek.

The sun was beginning to set when, at long last, they reached the wall of Truth-Will-Out Vine. Fig led them to the place that she and Milton had come through yesterday morning (how could it only be yesterday morning?). Even though everyone was beyond exhausted and even though it was not the triumphal return they had imagined, the thought of being almost home was as sweet as the scent of a SunBurst Blossom.

Rafi was leading the pack, and he only hesitated for a moment before stepping up to the shining green vines and wrapping a strand around one hand.

"I didn't want to move to this island," he said, "but now I'm kind of glad we did."

Just like last time, the hanging vines separated, pulling back to allow the four jungle explorers to move forward.

Gabe danced up next, a gap-toothed grin on his face. "I eat my boogers," he confided cheerfully as he threw his arms around the vines. "All of them. Always. Because they're delicious."

"Seriously, Gabe?" Fig said, and Milton was glad to see a tiny smile on her face again.

"That must be why the lemallabies liked you so much," Rafi said with a sigh. "You're basically one of them."

The vines seemed satisfied with Gabe's revelation. They parted again, and the four strode farther into the wall of vegetation.

When they reached the next layer, everyone paused. Milton knew they needed one more secret to get through, and he knew he should speak up because Fig probably wasn't in the mood to share.

But he didn't. As brave as he'd been on the riverbank, he was feeling decidedly less so now as he thought of everything his friends didn't know, everything he needed to tell them.

He felt both very relieved and very guilty when Fig moved forward. She twirled a green tendril in each hand. "For a while, I wasn't sure if I even wanted friends again," she said, "but now I know that I just needed to find the right ones."

She smiled at Gabe, then at Rafi, and finally at Milton. Milton beamed back at her, and the vines rustled and drew aside and the friendly leaves waved and the little flowers opened, tiny bursts of white, like stars coming out in the evening sky.

Then Milton saw that ahead of them were more vines.

Inside, his stomach was shriveling like a Menu-You Bush fruit in the sun. A teeny-tiny part of him whispered Fig's words: *What's the point of friends who only stick with you when you're happy and doing everything right?* Maybe she would stick with him, even though he'd done a lot of things wrong.

But another part of him was 99.99 percent sure that he was about to be flung back into Bird Brain territory.

Either way, the time had come to tell this truth. His friends had reached out their hands, and it was time for him to reach back, come what may.

"I have some very shocking news to reveal," he announced, his gaze fixed on the vines and only the vines. "And I hope we can still be friends after I share it." He took a long, shuddering breath. "I am not actually employed by the Triple F. And my name isn't really Sea Hawk. It's Milton." He lifted his chin and declared, "My name is Milton P. Greene."

Behind Milton P. Greene, there was silence. Then there came a *pshaw*.

He swung around to see Rafi shaking his head and smirking. Gabe was grinning too, although he looked mostly confused. Milton didn't know what kind of face Fig was making, because he was very intentionally not looking at her face. He wasn't ready for her verdict yet.

"What's so funny?" Milton demanded. "Aren't you shocked? Aren't you furious? I have revealed myself to be a liar. A charlatan. A fraud."

"I knew it!" Rafi cried. "I knew you were way too young to be employed by—well, by anyone. Plus, your binoculars are neon green with little cartoon seagulls on them."

"I didn't know," Gabe piped up. "I thought you were a pirate this whole time."

Milton finally got up the nerve to meet Fig's eyes. "Did you know, Fig?" he asked, wondering if this was the moment his *Restart* would finally end. Before she could answer, he rushed on: "I didn't mean to lie! Well, I did mean to lie. It was very much on purpose, and I know that was wrong. But it's just—it's just that I had the absolute worst year. It was the Most Totally, Terribly, Horribly, Heinously Rotten Year of All Time, and I wanted—I wanted to be someone else for a while. And it worked out extremely well. Sea Hawk found the field guide and sang to the centopus and climbed the Enmity-Amity Tree and saved you and everything!"

Fig's eyebrows were arched, but only a little. She put her arm around Milton's shoulders.

"Sea Hawk didn't do any of those things, you kook," she said, tipping her forehead toward his. "You did. This was your adventure, Milton P. Greene."

Inside, Milton was all ajumble, but that jumble didn't feel quite like it used to. He was achy and tender. He was nauseous and happy. He was rotten and spectaculous. He was, somehow, everything at once.

"Perhaps you speak the truth, my good friend," he said.

CHAPTER 63

Statues of Us

The Truth-Will-Out Vine split for the last time, and there was the banyan tree, somehow the same as when they left yesterday morning. The twisty-turny sea grape trees were the same too, and so was the field of wildflowers and palms the four walked through side by side (by side by side).

Milton's hiking boots had barely dried one bit, and when they reached the pebbly beach road, he paused to yank them off his feet. His socks were soaked too, and they smelled bad enough that he let out a *blergh!* when the odor caught his nose. His hiking clothes were nearly dry, but his whole backpack was heavy and sodden.

Because it had been underwater, which meant, Milton suddenly realized—

"My HandHeld!" he cried. "Sea Hawk!"

He yanked off his backpack, fell to his knees, and tugged the zipper open. From inside, he pulled out the dry bag and then his HandHeld and—

It was still dry.

"Is that what you play video games on?" Fig asked, leaning over him.

"I have one of those," Rafi said. "What games do you have?"

"I used to play *Isle of Wild*," Milton said, rising to his feet. "But I haven't been able to since my HandHeld ran out of battery power."

"So why didn't you charge it?" Rafi asked.

Milton wished he could raise his eyebrows like Fig because this question called for Maximum Arch Capacity. "Uh, because there's no electricity on the island," he said slowly.

"Not on this side," Rafi replied. "But they have electricity at the research station, obviously."

"Surely you jest!" Milton swung toward Fig. "Why didn't you tell me?"

Fig shrugged. "You never asked about the research station," she said. "I guess I assumed you knew."

"I did not know," Milton said. "I hadn't the slightest inkling."

He ran his fingers over the HandHeld's screen, over his own reflected face—his cheeks mud-smeared and his beautiful hat looking considerably worse for the wear. If he'd known that an out-let was only a (blergh-inducing) boat ride away, perhaps his time on the Lone Island would have been very different. Perhaps he'd be curled up on the couch-bed in Uncle Evan's house, crashing through virtual trees and rescuing virtual animals from injury and peril right now. Perhaps he would have spent the summer the way he had spent the rest of the year—feeling like a Bird Brain, pushing rotten thoughts to the back of his mind, wishing to be somewhere else and someone else.

But there was also this—*Isle of Wild* had given him a break from the rottenness of the year. Sea Hawk had shown him how to be brave and bold. And his adventures there—they had pushed him *onward, ever onward* in his adventures here in the real world.

"You can come to the station with me sometime and charge it if you want," said Rafi. "Dr. Greene let me set up a darkroom there so I can develop my photos. MY PHOTOS!"

"Egad!" Milton cried. Rafi was right next to him, and his voice at loud volumes really was all that a tone-deaf-loving centopus could ask for (and more).

Rafi had dropped *his* backpack now. "I took pictures of everything!" He pulled out a dry bag and removed his boxy camera. "Everything we saw—the Menu-You Bush, Little Smooshie Whatever, the Yes-No-Maybe-So Tree. I can develop them first thing tomorrow morning, and we can show Dr. Greene!"

Milton forgot about his HandHeld and *Isle of Wild*. He leaped to his feet and let out a bird-of-prey call as Fig caught him in a hug.

It was like finding the treasure for a second time. There were high fives and cheering and then a plan to develop the photos, and show Uncle Evan their proof.

And then there was Fig, running to the edge of the water, her buns undone and streaming behind her, her invisible backpack no longer weighing her down, shouting, "We're going to save you, island!"

Milton followed her down to the tide line and let his weary feet sink into the sand. Gabe cartwheeled down the dunes and then over to them, with Rafi trailing along behind him. The four of them stood together, listening to the rumble-and-hush of the waves and gazing up at the sunset-streaked sky. Milton knew they were unlikely to see an Astari Night Avis outside of the jungle, but the gleam of the stars would do fine.

When the Incredible Symphonic Cicadas began to play, Milton thought it was the most beautiful song he had heard yet. For a few melody-sweet moments, he thought that he would like nothing more than to stand on this beach with his friends forever. His feet would sink deeper and deeper into the sand. Seagulls would nest in his hair. Hermit crabs would nibble his toes. Eventually, they would become a part of the island, like salt-coated statues for future generations to marvel at.

Here they are, everyone would say. *The Lone Island Naturalists and Explorers Extraordinaire.*

He knew what happened after the cicadas' song, but still he stayed. He thought he could handle one or two mosquito bites in order to say goodbye to everyone. They had been through a lot together over the last two days, and he wanted to end their journey the right way.

Then the first mosquito bite came, and it felt like a Really-Sharp-Schnozzed Shrew was drilling into his jugular.

He couldn't handle it.

Milton took off down the beach, screaming, "So long, friends! Until tomorrow at six a.m.!" And then he was just screaming as the insects swarmed after him.

Uncle Evan was waiting inside the door with the heavy-duty fly-swatter. After he finished decimating the insects hitching a ride on his nephew, he said, "Milton—I mean, Sea Hawk—welcome home."

"Thank you, my good man," Milton said. He set his canvas back-pack down on the floor of the cottage. "It's good to be back. And it's quite all right if you call me Milton from now on. That's who I am."

CHAPTER 64

Hints & Promises

Milton hadn't felt so tired since he arrived at Uncle Evan's house nearly two weeks ago. He collapsed onto the stool at the driftwood table and inhaled some lukewarm spaghetti and meatballs (which actually wasn't as bad as he remembered). After a quick rain-barrel shower, he put on a clean T-shirt and shorts, groggily pushed the button that turned on his utility-belt watch's alarm, and staggered to his couch-bed.

Through it all, Uncle Evan said not more than five words. Being beyond exhausted, Milton wasn't exactly super chatty either, which was for the best since the plan was to totally blow Uncle Evan away by presenting all their jungle-findings at the same time tomorrow morning. Still, Milton couldn't begin his much-needed slumber without giving his uncle a hint of what was to come.

"Uncle Evan, I think you're going to be very happy tomorrow," he called from his facedown position on the couch-bed. "I mean, ecstatic. Probably the happiest you've ever been in your life."

"You think so?" Uncle Evan said.

"I do," Milton said. "I really, really do. So promise me one thing—promise you won't sign anything until you talk to me."

"Okay, Milt. Sure," was the last thing Milton heard before sleep as all-encompassing as a Menu-You Bush trap gulped him up.

CHAPTER 65

Missing! Take Two

It was sunshine and not his alarm that woke Milton the next morning. He rolled over and groggily held up his utility-belt watch.

Then he sat up sputtering and spitting! Water was pouring out of the watch face, and the hands were stuck at 5:47. Apparently it was not as waterproof as advertised.

Which meant the alarm had not woken him up at 5:30 a.m. as planned. The angle of the sun and the rising temperature in the cottage were a sure sign that it was much later in the morning. There was also silence behind the beaded curtain, which could only mean that Uncle Evan had already left for work at the research station.

BANG! BANG! BANG!

"AHHH!" Milton shrieked.

"Sea Hawk! I mean, Milton! Open up!" came Fig's voice from the other side of the front door. "It's almost nine o' clock!"

Milton leaped from the couch-bed and stumbled across the room.

"My alarm malfunctioned," he said, throwing open the door.

Fig was there, dressed in clean gear with freshly twisted-in-place buns. "I usually wake up without an alarm," she said, handing him a banana. "But I guess I was a lot more worn out than I realized. My mother finally woke me up because she wanted to hear how our campout went before she headed to the research station."

"I think Uncle Evan must already be over there," Milton told her. "Have you seen Rafi and Gabe?"

Fig started to shake her head when a voice called out, "Hey, where have you two been?"

Rafi and Gabe were coming up the path from the docks. "We've been awake since dawn getting these pictures developed," Rafi said, holding up a large folder and a roll of tape. "Let's go show your uncle!"

"I want my mother to see this," Fig said, starting down the porch steps. "She hasn't left our cottage quite yet—I'll get her and meet you at the docks!"

"At the docks? Why?" Rafi asked. "My parents are the only ones at the research station. Dr. Greene was there this morning, working on the computer, but he was gone by the time we came out of the darkroom. We figured he was here."

Uncle Evan wasn't at the research station. He wasn't at his cottage.

He was missing again!

But this time Milton knew exactly where his uncle, who needed to do a lot of thinking right about now, had gone.

"To Dr. Paradis's house!" he shouted, leaping from the porch.

They dashed down the pebbly beach road, with Fig taking a detour to bang on her sunshine door and yell, "Come to Dr. Paradis's quick!" They turned at the barely there trail, cut through the morning-sunlit dune-grass field, then raced into the shade of the tall trees that didn't seem nearly so tall now that they had scaled an Enmity-Amity Tree.

"Let's stick to the plan," Fig said, panting as they reached the clearing.

"Gabe and I can set it up here," Rafi agreed. "It'll only take a few minutes."

So Milton and Fig climbed the porch stairs of the dilapidated, dusty-musty onetime home of Dr. Ada Paradis. The door wasn't ajar this time. Milton turned the doorknob and Fig pushed. Together, they stepped over the threshold and traversed the dust bunny–filled, peeling-papered hallway until they came to the jam-packed sitting room.

There was Uncle Evan, seated at the rolltop desk, pen in hand, and a stack of papers in front of him.

CHAPTER 66

Caught Pen-Handed

"Cease and desist!" Milton bellowed so loudly and so intensely that dust scattered from every nearby surface, billowing around him in a very impressive cloud.

"Sea Hawk! I mean, Milton." Uncle Evan rose from the desk chair, putting the pen behind his back. "What are you doing here?"

"Uncle Evan, you said you would speak with me before signing anything, but I have caught you pen-handed," Milton said, pointing an accusing finger. "You lied!"

Uncle Evan sighed and dropped his hands to his sides. "I did," he said. "I wanted to get this over with."

There were footsteps behind them, and then Dr. Morris appeared in the doorway to the sitting room. She took in the scene silently, then nodded to Fig and leaned against the wall.

"Dr. Greene, we need you to listen to us," Fig said, turning from her mother.

If Uncle Evan had seemed unhappy before Dr. Morris arrived, he now looked utterly miserable. He was a slumped question mark of a man, and Milton could only hope that he would listen to the answers.

"All right," Uncle Evan said, giving a one-shouldered shrug. "But you should know that one night of observations from the tree ship is very unlikely to change the fate of this island."

"We weren't in the tree ship," Milton told him.

"We were in the jungle," Fig said, glancing at her mother, whose eyebrows popped up.

"And we found the proof you need," Milton said.

"Proof of what?" his uncle asked.

"Proof that everything Dr. Paradis told you about is still out there," Milton replied. "Proof that you shouldn't give up."

Uncle Evan studied them wearily for what seemed to Milton like twenty hours (he counted to ten at least two times). He didn't think he could wait for a second longer when from outside, there came a loud, screeching, bird-of-prey call.

It was the signal. Rafi and Gabe were ready.

"I'll have a look," Uncle Evan said. "But I'm sorry, I can't make any promises. Where's this proof?"

Milton nodded, his heart now thumping like the percussion section of a cicada symphony. He hoped Rafi and Gabe had done their job because it seemed like this was the last chance they were going to get.

"Right outside Dr. Paradis's front door," he said.

CHAPTER 67

Picture (Im)Perfect

It was exactly as they had planned.

Rafi's pictures were taped up all over the clearing. There **were** pictures on the oak trunks. There were pictures on the palm **fronds.** There were pictures spread out along the overgrown path. **There** were pictures hanging in the Truth-Will-Out Vine.

They should have been pictures of the Lone Island's **many** mind-boggling wonders—the remarkably leafed treescapes **and** the rainbow-hued blossoms, the briny-fruited Sweet Pickle **Tree** and the neon maw of the Menu-You Bush, the tentacle-frothed **river** and the letter-writing Yes-No-Maybe-So Tree and the bucktoo**thed** grin of a certain (disloyal) lemallaby.

They should have been pictures that would convince absol**utely** anyone and everyone that the Lone Island was a wild and **won-**drous place, a place worth protecting.

But something had gone wrong.

Well, it was *going* wrong, right before their very eyes. Each picture was at a different stage of fading into an indecipherable gray blur.

"I don't know what's happening." Rafi was standing in the middle of his smeary, monochromatic exhibit, looking frantic. "Maybe the photo paper got too hot on the supply-plane ride here or—or maybe I went too fast this morning and missed a step."

Milton felt like his sensitive stomach had been drop-kicked off the top of an Enmity-Amity Tree as he watched his uncle survey the scene from the porch. He didn't know what more he could do. He didn't know how to fix the pictures. More than that, he didn't know how to fix the disappointment that had weighed his uncle down bit by bit, year by year, as the Lone Island remained elusive and impenetrable.

As Uncle Evan turned back to the house, back to the desk, back to that terrible stack of papers, Milton's thoughts were tidal-waved by all the things he could not fix, by all the rottenness he could not get rid of.

He didn't know if he could fix his friendship with Dev—or if he even wanted to anymore. He didn't know if he would be able to speak up if those kids at school bullied him again or if they would even listen.

He didn't know how to fix his parents.

No matter what he did, there was always going to be some rottenness.

But then he remembered that he already knew that.

And he knew this: There was always going to be some spectaculousness too, even if it was sometimes as hard to find as a treasure hidden under the ground in the center of an island in the middle of the sea.

No, Milton couldn't fix everything, but he knew what he could do. He could keep going through the rottenness. He could keep searching for the spectaculous. He could call himself by his own name. He could make friends who would stick with him when he needed them most. He could believe in the message that his heart was pounding out again and again and again: *The adventure isn't over. The adventure isn't over.*

But how, how, how to get Uncle Evan to hear that same message?

Suddenly, from the corner of his eye, Milton saw a flash of teal. The Truth-Will-Out Vine on the sides of the clearing swayed in the breeze, and their rustling sounded like someone whispering a secret.

Milton had one last idea.

"Uncle Evan, I'll let you get right back to signing those papers without another word if you'll come with me for just a minute!" he cried.

Uncle Evan, in the doorway of Dr. Paradis's house, slowly turned back around. He looked tired. He looked defeated. He looked like a man who knew he couldn't fix things.

But he came down the steps and toward his nephew.

He dropped the pen.

And he reached out his hand.

Milton led his uncle around to the back of Dr. Paradis's house, to the place where he had first found the field guide. He positioned him right in front of the vines, so that the cords of brilliant green and the petals of blossoming white filled his vision.

"You told me that Dr. Paradis used to bring you here," Milton said, standing a little behind his uncle. "She wanted you to find the true Lone Island, and I know you think you've given up, but if you really had then you would have signed those papers and sent them right back. You didn't. You came here. To Dr. Paradis's house."

Uncle Evan reached out a hand again, this time to the Truth-Will-Out Vine. He ran his fingers along the wall of green that he had not been able to climb over or see through for all these years. "I came to the island with a plan," he said. "I was going to figure this place out, then move on to the next discovery. And when that didn't happen right away, I got discouraged." He shook his head, hands now winding through the vines. "I never really understood what Dr. Paradis was trying to tell me when we had our conversations back here. After she died, I worked harder and harder. I studied the vine, the cicadas, whatever wildlife I could find—but it always felt like I was missing something. I started spending less time outside and more time in the research station." He let out a

288

choky laugh. "Sometimes it feels like I've spent years hiding in that concrete building. Like I've been here, but not here."

"I know the feeling," Milton said to his uncle's hunched shoulders. "But you know, Dr. Paradis lived here for fifty years. It probably took her a super long time to understand the Lone Island too. And that something you were missing—that something Dr. Paradis was trying to show you—I think you still want to find it. And I think the island is still waiting for you to come out to meet it."

When Uncle Evan spoke, his voice was so soft that Milton could barely hear it. "I hope so, Milton," he said. "Because you're right. I've tried to give up, but I can't. Even after all these years, I still love this island, and I'm never going to stop trying to protect it."

Yes, Milton could barely hear his uncle, but it didn't matter. The words weren't for him anyway. They were for the Truth-Will-Out Vine, and the vine heard him loud and clear.

Under Uncle Evan's fingertips, the green strands began to move. He leaped back as they shivered and shook, then rolled up and spun out, leaves waving, flowers opening, the entire wall of vines seeming to dance and sway.

Then the vines went still.

There, lying on the ground, was the complete field guide and the satchel of samples that were supposed to be at the bottom of the sea.

CHAPTER 68

Never

The clearing was silent . . . for about two seconds.

"Great flapping falcons!" Milton cried. "How did the guide get here?"

"What's happening?" croaked Uncle Evan, staggering backward with one hand to his T-shirt-covered heart. "Why did the vines move? Everyone saw that, right?"

Dr. Morris's eyes were wide as she watched her daughter rush forward and pick up the guide. "Fig, what's going on?" she asked.

"I don't know how it got here," Fig said, facing her mother and Uncle Evan, "but this is why we went into the jungle."

"You found that in the jungle?" asked Uncle Evan. "But how? Where? Why?"

Fig glanced over at Milton, Rafi, and Gabe. Then she began: "Milton found a letter from Dr. Paradis right here behind her house."

"And Fig figured out the first clue that Dr. Paradis left inside," Milton continued, hurrying to stand next to his friend. "A clue that was supposed to lead us to a treasure."

"Then we spilled our guts to the Truth-Will-Out Vine and went into the jungle," put in Rafi as he and Gabe came over to Milton and Fig.

"Where we were almost killed like a bajillion times!" Gabe cried cheerfully. "There was a river monster and an invisible kitty cat and a plant that ate Milton, whadaya think about that?"

"The clues led us farther and farther into the island," Milton said. "Right to the thorn-shooting Enmity-Amity Trees."

"The Beautimous Lemallabies were at the top," Rafi continued. "And one of them—Lord Gnarly or something—led us to this all-knowing tree."

"Where we found this guide and these samples." Fig held up the guide so that Uncle Evan and her mother could read the cover, while Milton hefted the satchel with some difficulty. "I thought I lost them . . ."

"But somehow, they're here," Milton finished. "This is the treasure that will save the island."

The guide really was an enormous stack of very tightly bound (regurgitated) leaves. As Fig held it out to Uncle Evan (who kept glancing nervously at the rolled-up vine-balls), the leaf-pages flopped downward under their own weight and—

Something fell out.

"Another clue!" Gabe shrieked, pointing at the leaf-envelope that was now lying on the ground.

"A clue to what?" Fig asked. "We already have the treasure."

"Ask questions later," Rafi said. "Open it!"

Milton snatched up the envelope, thinking of the phlegmy-green one that had set all of this in motion not even three weeks ago. He didn't think he could read aloud because his stomach felt like an overly inflated centopus, so he handed it to Fig.

She opened it, removed several leaf-pages, and began to read:

Dear Guide Finder,

You've done it! You've found my guide, my samples, and a treasure that promises to be your greatest responsibility and your greatest joy.

When I arrived on the Lone Island fifty years ago, I was much like another young naturalist I know—ready to log more discoveries and continue making a name for myself. This island, I thought, was a challenge fit for an explorer like me.

But it took me many, many, many years to understand how this very unusual and very special place works and what it needed from me. As much as I wanted to share those remarkable truths with the world—and with that one young naturalist in particular—this adventure was my way of letting the island reveal itself.

If you are reading this, you have proved yourself truthful and open-

292

hearted, curious and thoughtful, brave and wise. You have proved that you are a true naturalist.

Yes, the Lone Island was waiting, and you came out to meet it with all you had. I can only hope that you continue to do so as you protect, explore, and share this island in the future.

Sincerely,

Dr. Paradis

Fig turned to the next leaf-page and continued:

"THE LAST WILL AND TESTAMENT OF DR. ADA PARADIS: I, Ada Paradis, explorer of islands, confidante of vines, befriender of creatures great and small, and the sole permanent resident of the Lone Island, being of competent and sound mind, do hereby declare this to be my last will and testament."

Fig stammered to a stop, eyebrows popping up to Maximum Arch Capacity as she realized what she had just read. "Here," she said, holding out the pages to her mother. "I think you should read this."

Dr. Morris took the letter and held it between her and Uncle Evan, who appeared thoroughly overwhelmed. Their eyes moved over the paper, and for a few minutes it was as if the entire jungle was holding its breath. There was no wind. The vines did not sway. There was no rustling in the bushes.

Inside Milton, there were one million and one thoughts, all of them jumbly, all of them mishmashed. He knew the young naturalist

293

Dr. Paradis had mentioned must be Uncle Evan. He knew that a will meant someone was getting something. But who and what?

"What does it say, Uncle Evan?" he finally blurted out, pressing his hat-covered head with both hands. "What's going to happen to the island? Is it still going to be sold to the Culebra Company? Did you inherit it?"

Uncle Evan shook his head, and Milton felt himself deflating like a serenaded centopus, sinking down.

"No, I didn't inherit the island," Uncle Evan said softly. "But Dr. Paradis did leave it to someone. Listen to this: *I give, devise, and bequeath all the remaining and residual property I have ownership in at the time of my death to the finder of this document, absolutely and entirely.*"

Fig pressed her hands to her mouth, while Rafi gaped and Gabe whispered, "Yowzers," but Milton shook his head.

"It's been quite the morning," he said. "Quite the year, in fact. Could you simplify that statement?"

Uncle Evan lowered the leaf-pages and smiled the biggest smile Milton had ever seen on any face anywhere.

"I didn't inherit the island, Milton," he said. "You did. You and Fig and Rafi and Gabe. You are the finders of this document, the finders of Dr. Paradis's will. You went out to meet the Lone Island, and now the Lone Island is yours."

Knees wobbling, Milton thought he might faint. He stumbled

backward into the wall of Truth-Will-Out Vine, letting the cords of green steady him.

"So I guess we should be asking you," Dr. Morris said, beaming at the four. "Are you going to sell the island to the Culebra Company?"

"Never," Fig said, flinging her arms around her mother.

"Never ever!" Gabe shrieked as he leaped onto his brother's back.

"Never ever ever," Rafi agreed.

Milton was about to add to this impromptu vote when behind him the vines began whooshing yet again—and then he almost fell over as the strands that had been holding him up swished away. He swung around to see that a second layer of vines had parted.

And sitting there, bushy tail twitching, round eyes shimmering, was the lemallaby formerly known as Little SmooshieFace—along with three dozen others. Each one had a SunBurst Blossom clutched in its paws, and each one was chitter-chattering with what sounded like happiness.

Uncle Evan staggered again, but this time he was moving forward. "Dr. Paradis told me about these!" he exclaimed. "Is that—is that Little SmooshieFace?"

"It's Lord Snarlsy," Milton corrected. "He didn't abandon me after all!"

Lord Snarlsy, holding a teal SunBurst Blossom, came leaping

out of the vines. He landed right on Milton's waiting shoulder and tucked the blossom behind his ear.

"How did you get here?" Milton asked him.

Lord Snarly chattered a response, but Milton (very disappointingly) still couldn't understand Lemallabese.

"He must have followed us this whole time," Fig said slowly. "That's what he was trying to tell us at the Yes-No-Maybe-So Tree. When he was pointing up, he was telling us that he wasn't going to walk."

"He came through the canopy," Rafi finished. "Like Dr. Paradis wrote in the entry, lemallabies don't travel on the ground."

"I knew this wacky kitty loved me!" Gabe sang out, his arms around his old chartreuse-bootied pal.

Milton nodded as the pieces came together, then gasped. "Lord Snarlsy, I saw you! Right before I was flung into the depths of the river. You must have seen Fig's backpack fall in and fished it out!"

Lord Snarlsy gave him a bucktoothed grin and a nod. The lemallabies behind him chattered their confirmation.

Finally, with his fauna friend perched on his shoulder, a Sun-Burst Blossom behind his ear, and a very full vest-covered heart, Milton P. Greene was ready to answer Dr. Morris's question.

"Are we going to sell the Lone Island?" he said. "Never. Never ever ever ever."

CHAPTER 69

An Adventure Like You Wouldn't Believe

It was a busy day, the day that Milton, Fig, Rafi, and Gabe found out they had inherited the Lone Island. There were lawyers to call and documents to scan and sign and send. There were more truths to tell, first to Uncle Evan and Dr. Morris, and then to the Alvarezes, who needed no convincing whatsoever and who were instantly as delighted as could be.

Yes, there were more truths to tell, but not *all*.

Uncle Evan didn't want to know everything. None of the scientists did. They wanted to meet the island on their own. With Milton, Fig, Rafi, and Gabe acting as hint-giving field guides, each was on their own expedition to part the vines and discover what lay beyond.

That, the friends had decided after many consultations with Dr.

Greene, Dr. Morris, and the Drs. Alvarez, was how they would continue to keep the island's flora and fauna protected.

Their plan was to turn the island into an international wildlife refuge. That way it would belong to everyone—but also to itself.

"Everyone who wants to do research or visit here will have to pass the island's tests," Fig said.

"Even if it takes them nine years," Milton agreed. "Even if it takes them a hundred."

There was plenty of time for conversations like these because Milton still had the rest of June, all of July, and the first week of August left on the Lone Island. He had time to go on dozens of expeditions into the heart of the jungle, to discover wildlife that wasn't on any Triple F Nature Sightings Checklist, and to be with his new friends.

Now that he knew there was electricity at the research station, he had time to charge his HandHeld too, but once he did, he never ended up turning it on. After finding that alive-right-here feeling, Milton didn't want to lose it again. He did use the satellite phone at the station though. Once a week, he dialed his mother's number and then his father's. It was hard to tell over the phone, but Milton thought they missed him, and he missed them too (when he had time to think about such things).

One afternoon, during the last week of July, Milton was heading back to Uncle Evan's cottage after a long day canoeing upstream (he and Rafi had their Tone-Deaf Warbler song down pat). The sky was getting ominously sunsetty, so Milton was double timing it to make sure he wasn't caught in another mosquito invasion. Before he could step up onto the cottage porch, he spotted two figures coming toward him from the docks.

Two faces that were strange in these surroundings, but as familiar as his own.

His mother and father.

For a moment, Milton stood frozen. He didn't feel one bit like a Bird Brain anymore, but seeing them here was a sudden reminder of all the totally, terribly, horribly, heinously rotten things that had happened that year. It was enough to stir his insides into the jumbliest of jumbles.

Then his mother started running toward him through the sand, and then Milton was running too. She caught him up in a hug so tight that the mishmash inside him seemed to be squeezing right back together.

"Look at you!" Milton's father cried once Milton's mother released him. "You look like an explorer."

Milton let his father hug him, and he felt that achy-tender-nauseous-happy mishmash smooshing together even more. He could feel the spectaculous mixed in there too now. It was spectaculous that his parents were here.

But there was also some rottenness they needed to deal with.

He counted to ten, wrapped in his father's arms. Then he pulled back and asked, "Are you divorced now?"

"Yes," Milton's mother replied.

"We are," Milton's father said.

"Okay," Milton said. "I guess I knew that." He adjusted his glasses and took a deep breath. "You know, I wasn't super happy about how things were going before I left. And I'm still not. It was a really rotten year for me. Truly."

"We know," his mother said, leaning down to find Milton's eyes under his hat brim, "and we're sorry. It was a hard year for us too, but we should have—we should have done better. For you."

"That's why we're here," his father added, gesturing around at the sand and the waves and the jungle beyond. "To spend time with you and to talk about this next year."

Milton didn't know exactly what they would talk about or how it would be spending time all together, but he noticed that his father didn't seem nearly as worn down and his mother didn't seem nearly as tense as they had before he left.

They both looked ready to be here, right here on the shores of the Lone Island.

So maybe it wasn't just Milton who was changing.

"As you know, I wasn't one hundred percent thrilled about leaving home for the summer," Milton told them as they climbed the porch steps. "But this trip turned out to be an adventure like you wouldn't believe. I discovered like a thousand new species, escaped death on numerous occasions, and saved the island from an environmental disaster. Well, my friends and I did."

"We want to hear all about it," his mother said.

"We sure do," his father agreed. "Tell us the whole story."

So Milton did.

CHAPTER 70

So Long, Milton P. Greene

Milton's parents stayed on the Lone Island for two weeks. During those two weeks, they swam in the bay and canoed in the river and met his friends and even made it behind the vines (although it took quite a lot of hint-giving on Milton's part). Milton could tell, at the end of each sun-soaked, salt-kissed day, that being there on the island, out in the wild, was as good for them as it had been for him. When they discussed plans for next year, *Weekend Park Expeditions* was at the top of Milton's list.

And then—quicker than he expected and sooner than he wanted—his time on the Lone Island came to an end.

On the last day, everyone gathered on the docks to say goodbye. Fig, Rafi, and Gabe were there, of course. So were Dr. Morris and the Drs. Alvarez. Lord Snarlsy wasn't there, but he had given Milton a super disgusting hairball to remember him by

(Milton had tried to act appreciative after he stopped feeling so blerghy).

"Before Milton goes," Uncle Evan told everyone, "I want to make a few announcements. First, I'm very pleased to share that the Drs. Alvarez have agreed to stay for another year."

The adults applauded and hugged, but Milton swung toward Rafi, anticipating grumpy-duck-faced fury. "You're staying?" he said. "Didn't you tell them how much you wanted to leave?"

Rafi, surprisingly, didn't look one bit furious. "I did, and they said we would go at the end of the summer. But then I realized that they weren't going to get to enjoy that twelve-legged spider or the giant butterfly or that beetle that turns itself inside out or any of the other insects behind the vines. So I told them we can stay." He grinned at Milton and shrugged. "I figure another year here might not be so bad."

Milton smiled back. He was glad Rafi was happy. He was glad Fig would not be alone . . . he was also insanely jealous. If only he could have more time on the Lone Island!

"Another announcement," Uncle Evan said, his voice as loud and strong as it had been during his visit to Milton's house seven years ago. "Dr. Morris, the Drs. Alvarez, and I have been talking, and we've decided to start a summer camp here on the island."

"Camp?" Milton balked. "I know you four are brilliant scientists, but have you really thought this through? You're going to let a bunch of kids roam through the centopus-and-UnderCover-Cat-filled jungle?

303

Forgive me for saying so, but egad! I'm truly questioning our choice to let you manage the island, Uncle Evan."

"It will be called the Naturalist and Explorer Extraordinaire Camp," Uncle Evan continued. "And during its inaugural summer, there will only be four campers."

Fig, Rafi, and Gabe cheered. It took Milton a moment (it was quite the pendulum swing of emotions), but when he understood, he cheered too.

He would be coming back to this place that felt so much like home.

And then it was time to go. Milton hugged Dr. Morris (who still called him Sea Hawk sometimes, which he didn't really mind) and the Drs. Alvarez (who gave him his second very disgusting souvenir— the molted exoskeleton of an Incredible Symphonic Cicada).

Rafi was next in the line of well-wishers. Looking anywhere but at Milton, he held out a package wrapped in newspaper (a completed word-puzzle page).

"Here," he said. "I got you a going-away present."

"That was incredibly thoughtful, Rafi," Milton told him. "Kind and sensitive and sweet. I always knew, even after you shook that fruit onto my head, that you had a soft side."

"Yeah, yeah, just open it," Rafi said.

Milton unwrapped the newspaper, slightly terrified that it might contain more bugs.

But it didn't. Inside was a pair of binoculars.

They weren't the very expensive, super high-tech Magnifycent2000s he had tried to persuade his parents to purchase for him. They also weren't neon-green plastic with seagull stickers.

They were somewhere in between.

They were perfect.

"Thank you, Rafi," Milton said, pulling Rafi into a hug that he allowed for two very nice seconds.

"You're welcome, Milt," Rafi said.

"Gotcha a present too, me hearty," Gabe sang. He thrust a large Yes-No-Maybe-So leaf-page into Milton's hands. Drawn there was a squashy sort of circle covered in triangles on sticks and squiggly lines and one big *X*.

"How magnificent," Milton said. "Very abstract."

"It's a treasure map," Gabe informed him.

"Oh, I see," Milton said. He rotated the leaf-page this way and that, squinting through his spectacles. "What does it lead to?"

Gabe laughed and spread his arms wide. "Here, of course," he said. "It'll lead you right back to the Lone Island. Right back to us."

"Of course it will," Milton said, trying not to blink his suddenly very full eyes.

Fig was last in the goodbye line. Milton didn't want to say goodbye to Fig, not ever.

He knew he had to though, and so he had spent an extraordinarily long time the night before trying to figure out how to say what

305

he wanted to say. He had composed a speech, in fact, about how she had lifted him from the mire of friendlessness and let him into her circle of Latin-name-knowingness and fearless-tree-climberly brilliance and about how her eyebrows alone were more eloquent than he could ever hope to be and how he would join her on a scientific expedition any day. It had been a truly beautiful speech.

But when he stood in front of her there on the dock, all Milton could manage was, "Great flapping falcons, I'm going to miss you!" before he burst into tears.

Fig studied him with wide, shiny eyes.

"It's a good thing you came here this summer," she said. "Otherwise, we would have lost our island. And I wouldn't have gotten to meet my best friend."

And then Fig hugged him.

And Milton P. Greene—former Bird Brain, son of now-divorced parents, failed karate student, cringe-and-weep-inducing singer, abysmal canoer, nearsighted, farsighted, short, skinny, friendless-until-just-a-few-months-ago—he had never been so happy to be himself.

"So long!" he yelled as Uncle Evan motored the little boat away from the dock. "Until next summer!"

"So long!" yelled Fig and Rafi and Gabe. "So long, Milton!"

It had been the Most Seriously, Supremely, Unexpectedly, Astonishingly Spectaculous Summer of All Time.

The Adridged Lone Island Field Guide
By Dr. Ada Paradis

Dear Guide Finder,

If you arr reading tis, I am dead, and the magnifycent island I have loved and comserved for fifty years is in terrible janger.

Put feer not! Somewhere in the jumgle, I have left vou a treesure that will keep the Lone Islard prodected and fwee. To find this treasure, yoo will have to follow dhe clues along the way and wittin the pagez of this field guide. If you succeed, yuu will have broven yourself to the island and truly earnud the treasure and all it entails.

So off you go, Guide Finder, on a wild and wonderous adventure. The Lone Island awaits!

Simcerely,

Dr. Ada Paradis

Table of Contents

Truth-Will-Out Vine

Where else could you start but at the Truth-Will-Out Vine? This epiphytic plant may be the most misunderstood of the Lone Island flora. Not a destroyer but a protector, the vine's unique survival adaptation is the island's first line of defense. It has stood firm (or hung firm, rather!) against many would-be Lone Islanders with questionable intentions over the years. If you want to find the treasure, you will first have to go back and decode the truth about the Truth-Will-Out Vine. Then go forward to tell your own, which, if you have found this guide, you have already begun to do.

Habitat: Forms a dense perimeter around the island's interior

Population Estimate: Millions and millions of strands

Disposition: Perhaps a tad overcautious, but always willing to listen to those who have nothing to hide

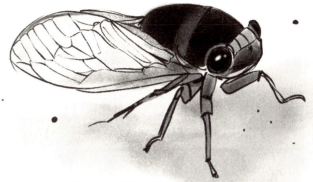

Incredible Symphonic Cicadas

These little buggies are jet-black with white wings, like they're wearing teeny-tiny tuxedos. Every summer, they come topside to play their original compositions by vibrating their tymbals in concert. How these creepy-crawlies can sound like an angelic choir, I may never truly understand, but their melodies are magnificent. Unfortunately for them, they are a favorite snack of many Lone Island fauna. In fact, in my experience their emergence is the perfect time to explore the island since many predators will have full tummies and thus be less likely to, you know, eat you.

Habitat: Out of sight, out of reach, but always within earshot, the cicadas live beneath and within the Truth-Will-Out Vine

Population Estimate: Seems like a billion gazillion in the summertime

Disposition: Moody musician types

Food Source: Aboveground, these cicadas mostly sip on the sap of the Truth-Will-Out Vine, but they will swarm and drain a Sweet Pickle Tree dry, so gaga are they over its puckered fruits

311

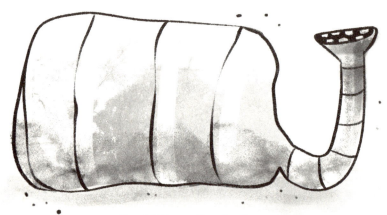

EarthWorm Pachyderm

Elephants may never forget, but EarthWorm Pachyderms suffer from permanent amnesia. These wiggling lumps of blubber squirm aimlessly through the earth by means of an extremely long, dirt-inhaling proboscis. Chunks of stone go in their snouts and sand comes out . . . well, the other end. Fully grown they are about twelve feet in length, plus up to five feet of trunk. The EarthWorm Pachyderm has no natural predators, but their numbers are kept in check by frequent cave-ins of their tunnels. When an animal the size of a rhinoceros is lumbering around underground, it's bound to get squashed quite a lot.

Habitat: Subterranean

Population Estimate: My best guess is a dozen or so although there may be more deeper in the earth

Disposition: Touchy and, to put it politely, not terribly bright

Food Source: Dirt and rock candy

Really-Sharp-Schnozzed Shrew

This shrew "nose" how to get down! Ha! A little levity for you! The Really-Sharp-Schnozzed Shrew is a tiny creature with a corkscrew nose that spins like a drill. This unique facial feature allows the rodent to tunnel through the soil and bedrock of the island in search of its favorite snack, Incredible Symphonic Cicada larvae. Weighing just half a pound, the shrew can eat up to five hundred larvae a day! A fun fact: The Really-Sharp-Schnozzed Shrew and the EarthWorm Pachyderm are not overly fond of each other and have been known to have "nose-offs," where each attempts to murder the other using only its honker as a weapon.

Habitat: Subterranean

Population Estimate: Around two hundred full-schnozzed adults and their mini-schnozzed offspring

Disposition: Hardworking, but tunnel-visioned

Food Source: Worms, grubs, and larvae . . . to each their own, I suppose

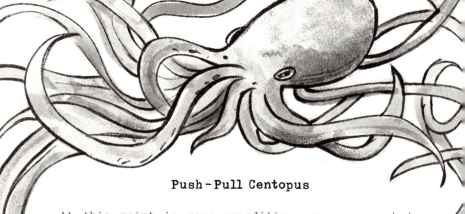

Push-Pull Centopus

At this point in your expedition, you may want to learn more about this river-dwelling creature. The Push-Pull Centopus has a small, rubbery body with one hundred tubelike legs, each ending in a suction-cup appendage. Highly territorial, the centopus will suck river water in through these legs, swelling its stretchy little body up like an elephantine beach ball, then spew out every last drop at potential intruders. This push-pull sequence is very beneficial for the island, acting as an irrigation system as the river water is forced through the tunnels created by the Really-Sharp-Schnozzed Shrew and the Earth-Worm Pachyderm. It does, however, make canoeing quite challenging, but here's a hint: The serenade of the Tone-Deaf Warbler lulls the centopus into a peaceful slumber, thus shutting off the waterworks.

Habitat: Deepest parts of the river

Population Estimate: Up to five Push-Pull Centopuses lurking in the murky depths

Disposition: Generally sucky, but serene when the Tone-Deaf Warbler is nearby

Food Source: Marshwiggle Weeds, Itty Bitty Fish, and whatever else it happens to inhale

Tone-Deaf Warbler

To "warble" is to sing in a soft, low, pleasing fash-
ion, and most warblers do indeed warble this way. The
Tone-Deaf Warbler, however, is the indubitable excep-
tion. With a magenta beak and shimmering gold plumage, the beauty of this fine-feathered friend often
lures admirers closer. Don't be pulled in! That bright
beak can unleash a song so shrill and so shriekingly
horrendous that it clears the jungle for a two-mile
radius. For your ears' sake, keep earplugs handy if
you spot their nesting trees. But again, remember: As
odious as the sound is to human ears, the song of the
Tone-Deaf Warbler is a sweet, sweet lullaby to the
Push-Pull Centopus.

Habitat: Nests in the branches of the Bristly Thistly
Bush

Population Estimate: Over fifty at last count (which
was quite a while ago . . . I had a headache for two
weeks after that one)

Disposition: Joyful, but lacking in self-awareness

Food Source: Mostly insects, but will pick at the
odd Itty Bitty Fish that the Push-Pull Centopus spits
its way

Astari Night Avis

One of the Lone Island's camouflaged critters, the Astari Night Avis is a light-shunning, nocturnal bird. Its entire body—skin, feathers, and guts—is translucent and colorless by day. When the sun GOes down, the Avis becomes an inky-black canvas of moon, stars, and comets. It has been said that any wish made on a shooting star spied in the tail feathers of an Astari Night Avis will come true. Of course, I am the originator of that saying and the only one who has ever seen such a thing, so maybe that's just wishful thinking on my part. But maybe not.

Habitat: Soaring through jungle canopy or nesting in the Starlight Starbright Trees, which incidentally, are the perfect trees to spend the night under

Population Estimate: Maybe twenty or so? They're practically invisible so that's a total guess

Disposition: Secretive, silent, spectacular

Food Source: Moon rays and Milky Way Beetles

Menu-You Bush

The Menu-You Bush was discovered when a famished explorer (who shall not be named) broke the cardinal rule of foraging: Never eat an unknown fruit. Luckily, she chose the fluorescent-orange-and-pink-striped fruit of the Menu-You Bush, which somehow (don't ask me how) tastes exactly like whatever the cuisine the eater wants most. It certainly makes the perfect dinner for weary jungle trekkers. But beware! This carnivorous plant (not the only one around, by the by) uses its fruit TO lure prey into its jawlike leaf-trap. Like its diminutive cousin the Venus fly-trap, the Menu-You Bush will begin digesting its prey after five movements. The trap cannot be pried open from the outside, so if you happen to be on the Menu-You's menu, act with speed and deliberation and apply pressure to the petiole!

Habitat: On the banks of freshwater sources

Population Estimate: Abundant and ravenous

Disposition: This bush is frightful, but its fruit is delightful!

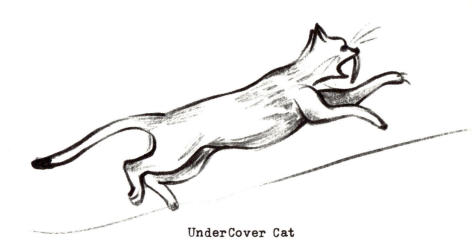

UnderCover Cat

This feline is rarely spotted, even by the keenest observer (of course, I'm referring to myself). Its fur is made up of a complex arrangement of reflective hairs. As a result, the UnderCover Cat is almost completely camouflaged. The only unmirrored parts are the cat's retractable fangs, which are a foot long and razor-sharp. Full-grown, these cats weigh around four hundred pounds. They can leap to the top of an Enmity-Amity Tree in a single bound and reach speeds of up to one hundred miles per hour. So if you see two floating fangs coming toward you—yes, you should be afraid. Be very afraid! But also—you're on THE right track. If you're still in one piece, keep going!

Habitat: Near the center of the island

Population Estimate: Around eight full-grown Under-Cover Cats and their offspring on the island at any given time

Disposition: Honestly, kind of terrifying

Food Source: Various small mammals . . . and intruders

Enmity-Amity Tree

When you reach these trees (and I hope you do reach them), you'll know it. Up to three hundred feet in height, each squared-off trunk is covered in hundreds of holes, about an inch in diameter each. One of two things can come out of those holes: (1) little wooden branches that you can use to climb the tree (yay, Amity!), or (2) poisonous thorns that will kill you on the spot (yikes, Enmity!). Want the Amity option? Of course, you do! Here's what you need to know: (1) Each of the tree's four sides must be pressed simultaneously, and (2) all tree-touchers must have amity between them. Like the Truth-Will-Out Vine, this flora's sensitivity to the reactions and intentions of would-be climbers is a survival adaptation. Little SmooshieFace and two delightful Oddest of Odd Otters were my companions on my first trip up, and while it was extremely nerve-racking even for an intrepid explorer such as myself, it was worth the climb. Well worth it.

Habitat: Even nearer to the CENTER OF THE ISLAND

Population Estimate: Copse of thirty trees

Disposition: The best bud you'll ever have or a murderous lunatic . . . it's up to you!

SunBurst Blossoms

What a beautiful morning it is when you are surrounded
by SunBurst Blossoms! These enormous flowers can be up
to six feet in diameter, but they're usually devoured
by the Beautimous Lemallabies long before they get
that big. With a round center and twelve overlapping
petals fanning out, each blossom has a unique, brilliant hue. Like the Truth-Will-Out Vine, this plant
is an epiphyte, growing on a tree rather than being
rooted in the ground, and it likes to be as high up as
possible. The blossoms bloom every morning at first
light and close up every evening at sundown.

Habitat: Soakin' up the sun

Population Estimate: Abundant . . . unless the lemallabies are having their Annual Summer SunBurst Munch-
Fest

Disposition: Morning-lovers, very antisocial at night

Beautimous Lemallaby

Of all the fantastic flora and fauna I have found here on the Lone Island, this little critter is my absolute favorite. Remember your taxonomy? Kingdom, phylum, class, order, genus, family, species? Well, the Beautimous Lemallaby isn't just a new species. It's a brand-new class—a sort of marsupial/rodent/primate mishmash and an extraordinarily advanced one at that. Each lemallaby has a unique SunBurst Blossom pattern on its rump, which serves as camouflage as they travel through the jungle canopy, never setting their adorable little toesies on the ground. I am so fond of the lemallabies, in fact, that I have named one of them Little SmooshieFace because of his adorable visage, and he has become my greatest confidante and adviser on island matters. Yes, Little SmooshieFace knows it all.

Habitat: That's for me to know and you to find out by studying this guide from start to finish

Population Estimate: Fifty-six lemallabies at last count

Disposition: Brilliant, funny, adorable, just the absolute best

Food Source: SunBurst Blossoms, all day every day

Yes-No-Maybe-So Tree

The Yes-No-Maybe-So Tree is the most remarkable and most knowledgeable of all the Lone Island's endlessly fascinating flora. The leaves of this possibly omniscient tree are rectangular, cream colored, and very thin. The seedpods are long, pointed at the tip, and ooze a black sap. Many of my field notes (even those in your hands at this very moment) have been written on these paper-leaves. And as if that were not amazing enough, the Yes-No-Maybe-So Tree will also answer any question—although it can only respond (you guessed it) *Yes*, *No*, or *Maybe So*. By now, I'm sure you can think of a few questions to ask, can't you?

Habitat: Super top secret

Population Estimate: One single solitary tree

Disposition: I once wrote, *Are you a happy tree?* and the Yes-No-Maybe-So Tree wrote back, *Yes*. So there you have it.

Food Source: Mostly sunshine but the tree may ingest—and possibly regurgitate—the occasional stacks of paper-leaves and more

Acknowledgments

All my thanks to everyone who went on this wild and wondrous adventure with me, including:

My spectaculous agent, Sara Crowe, who blazed a trail for this story with Sea Hawkian vim and vigor.

My super amazing editor, Janine O'Malley, a WordSmith and story-decoder of the highest order.

My super fantastic assistant editor, Melissa Warten, who reads with Magnifycent2000 vision.

Cassie Gonzales, whose art and design are like a wish (made on a shooting star in the tail feathers of an Astari Night Avis) come true.

Matt Rockefeller, who somehow outdoes himself on each cover. I mean, seriously. Egad!

The entire team at FSG and Macmillan Children's, including Jen Besser, Madison Furr, Katie Quinn, Katie Halata, Hayley Jozwiak, Chandra Wohleber, Sarah Chassé, Mary Van Akin, and many more. It's a joy to trek through the jungles of publishing with you all.

Holly McGhee, Elena Giovinazzo, Ashley Valentine, Cameron

Chase, Rakeem Nelson, and David Ford. A Pippin expedition is the very best expedition!

Brigid Misselhorn, for being the kind of early reader and friend that every author dreams of.

Teachers, librarians, booksellers, fellow authors, and story lovers—I continue to be honored and amazed by all the supportive, enthusiastic helping hands on the kidlit community Amity Tree.

My readers, who are, to quote Dr. Paradis, *Brilliant, funny, adorable, just the absolute best.*

My parents, who helped me learn how to move through the rotten and find the spectaculous. Thank you for loving Milton—and me—from page one.

Russ, who has explored oceans, mountains, jungles, and rivers with me. Let's go on adventures together forever.

And as always, to Coral Mae and Everett Reef. You two are my Most Seriously, Supremely, Unexpectedly, Astonishingly Spectaculous Adventure of All Time. Great flapping falcons, I love you both so much!